MISSION: RED SCYTHE

C.W. JAMES

MISSION: RED SCYTHE

Copyright © 2025 by C.W. James.

For information contact:

Insundry Productions Books, Gardnerville NV 89460

insundryproductions.com

ISBN (ebook): 978-1-962056-09-0

ISBN (paperback): 978-1-962056-10-6

Library of Congress Control Number: 2025906869

Also by C.W. James

The Treasure of Peril Island
Brothers Three
Mindfield
The Tomb of Ptahmes

Special Thanks to
Edgar Wallace

All the gadgets mentioned in the text were developed and/or deployed by various intelligence services from the World War II era through the 1960s. Some devices were slightly modified to fit the story, but maintained the technology available during the period.

James Vagus pushed open the door to his dorm room and stepped inside. He tossed his diploma folder and program onto the bed. The cover read *St. Michael's Academy for Boys 1965 Graduation Ceremony* in a suitable formal typeface. While he sat in the stuffy auditorium during the proceedings, he grew bored with the never-ending speeches and checked for his name. It was listed way back on page 8... the curse of having a surname starting with a letter toward the end of the alphabet.

Loosening his tie, he scanned the small room — his home for the past six years. A single, not very comfortable bed, an overloaded bookcase, a compact metal desk with a lamp, a chair, and a wardrobe. Spartan. He never added homey touches. Never saw the point. He had no family photos to display, anyway.

In only two weeks, he had to move out, but he had no idea where he would go. The thought of applying for a job at the Academy crossed his mind again. That would provide him with room and board, but he also knew it would drive his teachers and counselors crazy. They all assumed he would pursue higher education, "since he was such a bright young man." He was pulled aside many times during the past year — even up to the very morning of the ceremony — to engage in "little chats" about it.

But the truth was, James had no intention of going to college or had any plans for his future at the moment. Of course, he listened to the adults politely, told them he appreciated their concern, but this bright young man had no bright ideas about his future.

He took off his jacket and hung it up in the wardrobe with great care. He didn't have many clothes, so he had to make the ones he had last. Plopping down on the uncomfortable mattress, he loosened his tie as he gazed at his diploma. There it was: the result of twelve years of schooling. It was supposed to be a significant achievement, something to be proud of and shared... but for him, it was only another piece of paper. Albeit a fancy printed one.

James stood, moved to the window and opened it, letting a rush of warm, humid air fill the room. He watched families clustered in the courtyard below, their faces glowing with joy, their voices a chorus of celebration. Cameras flashed, capturing moments that would be enshrined in photo albums and memories for years. A little boy ran across the grass, waving a mortarboard too large for his small hands. A man scooped him up, ruffling his hair, and the boy's giggles echoed upward.

James stared at them for a long moment. He gripped the sash, ready to slam the window shut, lock out all the loud noise of family happiness — then he paused, breathing deep, forcing down the resentment. He was working hard not to be bitter. Turning his back on the scene outside, he tried to block out the sounds of a life he never knew.

From his pocket, he pulled a small felted blue jewelry box and opened it. Inside, a small sterling silver cross gleamed. He smiled, rubbing the cross between his thumb and forefinger, feeling its cool, smooth contours. The sisters from the orphanage attended the graduation, and seeing their familiar, kind faces in the crowd meant more than he could express. They were the closest thing to a family he ever had.

He took the cross and held it up, letting it catch the light. Slowly, he draped it around his neck, the metal settling against his chest with a comforting weight. He touched it again, vowing to himself that he would never remove their gift.

There was a knock, startling him. James turned toward the door. "Come in."

A middle-aged man stepped into the room. He was a little shorter than James, who stood at six feet tall. His hair had begun to show hints of gray, and he wore a well-fitted pinstripe suit. He entered the room with an air of authority, but otherwise possessed an unremarkable appearance. Put him against a blank wall, and he'd blend in seamlessly. James did not recognize his visitor at all.

"I would like to congratulate you on your graduation," the man said.

"Thanks." James studied him, trying to place the face. Nothing. "Mister...?"

There was no answer. Instead, the man looked around the room and walked over to the bookcase. He ran a finger along the spines. "You have quite a collection of foreign language books."

"I speak four languages fluently, and four more to some degree. Whenever an overseas sister came to the orphanage, I pestered her until she taught me her native language." James shrugged. "I guess I have a facility for it."

The man turned, hands in pockets. "I would say that was more than a mere facility."

James was still at a loss to what the man wanted, or who he was. Did the guy wander into the wrong room? "I'm sorry, I didn't catch your name." He waited, curious, wary. The visitor appeared to be somebody important, but why the mystery?

"Why didn't you accept the valedictorian honor when it was offered?" the man asked, ignoring James' hint.

"I thought it should go to someone whose family could share in the pride," James answered before realizing it wasn't the man's business at all.

"Interesting," the man said, more to himself than James. He then studied James like he was a piece of abstract art hanging in a museum, trying to determine the painting's subject.

"How did you know about that?" James demanded.

The man flashed a tight smile, as though his lips were out of practice. "Let's say it's a privilege of the one paying the bills."

"Paying the bills..." James repeated. His brow furrowed in confusion. Was this man some type of anonymous benefactor revealing his existence? Was he about to yell "Surprise! I'm your lost rich uncle!" James shook his head slightly in confusion. "Wait... are you saying... I thought I was here on a full scholarship."

"You were." He walked to the window. "Of sorts."

"Of sorts? What does that mean? Are you telling me you picked up the tab for the past six years?" James asked.

"To respond to your last question — no, I personally did not pay your tuition. However, I represent the organization that did." The visitor looked over the school grounds.

"I'm sorry... who are you again? What's this 'organization'?" James took a couple of steps toward the man.

The man met James' gaze as he turned to him — steady, steely. "Smith. My name is John Smith," came the response after a brief pause, almost as if he was thinking up an alias on the spot.

The answer seemed flung like a challenge, as if the man was testing James' reaction to such an obvious lie. James was tempted to respond with a sarcastic "you've got to be kidding", but decided not to.

Perhaps this man was some type of eccentric millionaire who bankrolled James' education, and this was some weird rite he liked to perform. James supposed people like that could exist and figured he had enough time to play along. After all, he was not expected at any post-graduation parties. His tone implied that he was aware the name was false, but he accepted it — for now. "A pleasure to meet you, Mister... Smith."

Smith nodded, as though James had passed a test. "At least that's the name I'm using for the present time," he said without a trace of irony or explanation. He went to the desk and sat in the chair. James took a seat on the bed.

James' gaze remained locked on the man sitting across from him as memories pulled him back to the orphanage. There, he learned the craft of careful observation and subtle adaptation in order to please potential adoptive parents. Now, as he sat on the edge of the bed, James couldn't shake the feeling that he was once again being judged and evaluated. And he automatically was again playing that same game, mirroring his visitor's every move, analyzing words used and body language, engaging in a mental chess match. But this time, he wasn't sure if he wanted to please or deceive. But it was clearly his turn.

"How very interesting. What kind of organization?" James asked. "The one I can thank for the open checkbook."

Smith's cool demeanor remained unchanged. "The world has been split into two halves after World War II. There is now intense geopolitical tension between the United States and its NATO allies, representing Western capitalist democracies, and the Soviet Union and its Eastern Bloc allies, representing communist states."

"I know. I got an 'A' in Social Science," James said. "What does —"

The visitor went on. "Then you are aware there is a fierce ideological struggle between capitalism and communism. This Cold War has permeated global politics, economics, and cultures. So far, direct military confrontation has been avoided, but both superpowers seek to extend their influence globally. While avoiding shooting at each other, the two sides engage in proxy wars, nuclear armament races, and intense espionage."

"Yes, and..." James prompted.

Smith spoke after a moment's silence. "The group of which I am a member is part of that struggle."

James folded his arms across his chest and grinned. He volleyed the ball back. "Sounds like you're talking about the CIA."

The reply erased his smile.

"Same league, different team," Smith said. "The CIA personnel are quite capable, but may at times have experience difficulty entering certain locales because of their higher average age. It was proposed that a smaller agency consisting of younger operatives could be of assistance in certain cases, and handle some basic surveillance tasks. This would free older agents for other missions."

"Like a squad of boy secret spies?" James raised an eyebrow.

"Not exactly." Smith paid no attention to the sarcasm. "A male needs to be 18 years old to join the military without parent or guardian permission. So youngsters serving as spies are the stuff of fiction. But there is a need for younger agents, particularly in infiltrating specific areas. Colleges, rock concerts, clubs, that kind of scenario. It is assumed these youthful operatives would be useful for approximately five years or so. Although as long as they can pass for somebody younger than their actual age, the service length could be extended. For example, your blonde hair, blue eyes and boyish looks could lead to a longer career."

James nodded in appreciation of the compliment. "And when they become old and wrinkled, they're put out to pasture? Or are they merely shot?"

"None of that," Smith dismissed. "The agents will be offered a choice to either retire from the organization with their country's gratitude and a generous pension, or transfer to a different agency — the CIA. I am a part of what is known as MIS-X. Originally, it was a secret military intelligence unit formed in World War II to help Allied prisoners escape Axis prison camps. Although it was inactive after the peace, it was never officially disbanded. Like most government programs, it existed in some form, if only in a folder residing in a file drawer. Now, MIS-X is being reconstituted to train and deploy young agents for a new purpose."

"It would be a shame to waste all that stationary," James remarked dryly.

"Indeed," Smith said in sincerity. James concluded his visitor had no sense of humor.

"MIS-X has been in an organizational and planning mode," Smith went on. "It has spent several years locating, monitoring, and sometimes, providing support for hundreds of children who we projected could fill our staff."

James aimed his dart. "Sounds like you've been raising prize hogs, waiting for them to get fatter for slaughter." There was no reaction. "Am I safe to believe I was I one of those 'monitored and supported' children?"

Smith nodded.

"I trust I've been an interesting subject," James returned.

Smith shrugged. "About average."

"And now you've come for your pound of flesh?" It was more of a statement than a question.

"A nice Shakespearean allusion... *The Merchant of Venice*. Act Three, if I remember," Smith said.

"Act Four," James corrected. "Shylock was unsuccessful in his quest."

A flicker of approval appeared in Smith's brown eyes. "Yes, you are correct." He flashed another tight smile. "But no, that is not my purpose here."

Memories from the orphanage again intruded into James' mind. Of all those meetings with prospective parents, the trying for approval from them, for adoption by them, followed by crushing disappointment. A surge of anger he couldn't control, the anger of never being chosen, of always wondering why he wasn't good enough, why no family wanted to adopt him, flared. He jumped up and strode to Smith. His eyes narrowed as he jabbed his index finger at his visitor. "Did your 'monitoring' derail those potential adoptions of me that fell through?"

Smith rose, his actions precise and controlled. He stood with his weight evenly distributed on both feet, arms held at his sides. James couldn't help but think it appeared Smith was expecting a violent response from him... or perhaps he was testing James' reaction to that idea.

"No. We did not influence those." Smith spoke in a quiet voice, maintaining eye contact with James. "It's more likely that you intimidated the couples."

"Intimidated them?" James sputtered.

Smith relaxed his stance. "Most people seeking to adopt don't want a child who is far more intelligent than they are."

"Is that supposed to be a compliment?" James fired back.

Smith remained unruffled. "No, simply an observation. At any rate, your adoption status would have made no difference to us. We still would have communicated with you at this time, although families complicate matters."

Silence settled over the room. James stared hard at Smith, the man's calm, calculated presence gnawing at him. Smith continued to observe James with an intense gaze, as if he were assigning points for different aspects and then tallying the total. Finally, he gave a slight, almost imperceptible nod. "I think you have potential."

James unclenched his fists, not realizing he'd balled them up. "Potential?"

"Based on my observations and your school record, you have the foundations to join us. MIS-X is now ready to enter its operational stage, although experimental — a trial — at first. A small operation with a limited number of agents. I am offering you a slot in the first training class," Smith said.

James couldn't believe what he was hearing. Just moments ago, he didn't have an idea about his future. Now, he was being offered the opportunity to become a secret agent — it was all too much to take in. There most likely be possibility of injury... or worse. Did he

want to risk becoming involved in that type of life? "I...
I need some time to think about this..."

"Understandable," Smith replied. "You do not have
to decide immediately."

"And if I say no?" James asked.

"You're under no obligation to accept, of course."
Smith answered. "We will never force anyone to join
the organization. A coerced operative is a dangerous
and unpredictable one. You are free to live a life of
your own making. With or without service to MIS-X."

James gestured around the room. "And all the money
you've spent on my education?"

"Consider it a scholarship, as you called it. You do
not need to repay." Smith adjusted his suit with a flick
of his wrists. He extended his hand. James shook it.
"Remember, your age is crucial to the MIS-X mission,
so my offer is only open for two weeks. The training
program starts in a month and a half. We have other
possible recruits to contact in the meantime. If you
wish to join, you can stay at the decommissioned military base we're using without cost until we begin."

As he turned to leave, he cast a look at James' slender build. "There are excellent weight lifting facilities
there." He placed a business card on the desk. "You can
call this number when you decide. Again, congratula-
tions on your graduation, James. I hope that you will
become part of MIS-X."

The door closed with a soft click. James stood motionless, the room's silence pressing in on him, stunned at the interview he just went through. He tried to understand what just had occurred, the wholly unexpected choice offered to him. After a few minutes, he walked to the desk and picked up the card. It was blank, other than a single phone number, centered and printed in crisp, black ink.

Tapping the card against his thumb, James stared after Smith.

Chapter One

J AMES STEPPED OUT OF the luxurious Ocean View Resort onto the expansive pool deck. It dissolved into the sandy beach that lay just beyond. The relaxing area was adorned with plush cabanas, inviting loungers, and towering palm trees providing pockets of shade from the Miami heat. The blazing sun cast a golden light over the sparkling waves of the Atlantic, creating a shifting display of flashing colors.

He was excited finally to travel some place new. Something different from the monotonous Greyhound bus trips he took through endless corn fields between the orphanage and the Academy. During the taxi ride from the airport, he almost pressed his nose against the window like a small child, eager to take in the sights of the vibrant Florida city. He drank it all in — the shimmering ocean, the charming, pastel-colored art déco buildings, and the lush, tropical greenery.

Beneath his excitement, though, lay deep-seated nervousness. MIS-X's ten-month training was grueling. Physical conditioning, self-defense and weapons instruction, various gadgets and gizmos to learn, current affairs lectures... a dozen of his fellow fifty recruits had been weeded out or quit along the way. Several times, James wanted to tell the demanding Smith where he could put MIS-X and stalk away, but he didn't. He completed the course — barely — and was proud of that accomplishment.

He was an 18-year-old, he told himself, about to step on the dangerous chessboard of international intrigue in the middle of the Cold War waged between two superpowers. Not only that, but he couldn't throw out the sense of fear and doubt as he began his first mission. Was he ready for this? Would he be able to handle the pressure and risks involved? Should he have taken Smith's offer at all? But there was no time for second guessing about that now. He was all in. Deep.

The shouts and laughter of the swimmers mixed with the nagging squawks of seagulls as James looked around. The commotion provided a perfect cover, a carousel of playful chaos helping him move unnoticed. He scanned the area until his gaze zeroed in on his target: Otto Stardt. James had thoroughly studied the German's dossier and committed every detail of his background to memory.

The heavyset businessman lounged under a large umbrella, exposing a tiny sliver of his body to the sun. It was a perfect picture of his preferred shady dealings, James mused. Stardt reclined on a striped beach chair like a king surveying his kingdom. James couldn't help but wonder if it was under this guise of leisure that Stardt was dreaming up more of his notorious business affairs. From a distance, James could sense Stardt's cautious demeanor and how his eyes constantly scanned the surroundings — indications of a man with many secrets to conceal.

The assignment was a routine one: to monitor Stardt's movements and contacts. International intelligence agencies had been keeping an eye on the businessman since the end of World War II, and now it was James' turn at bat. Two hours passed since his arrival in Miami, and he already completed his initial tasks inside the hotel. Now it was time to get closer to his target.

James surveyed the crowded beach. His eyes darted from the sunbathers to the children playing in the surf, then back to Stardt. He needed to remain invisible, just another student in pursuit of the American dream of a seaside vacation and a golden tan. He allowed himself a small smile. Blending in was an art, he had been instructed, and he was determined to become its master.

He spotted an empty lounger within radio range of the German businessman. A quick scan assured him no prying eyes were fixed on him. With sunglasses perched on the bridge of his nose, James stepped onto the sand.

James' nerves were on edge. This was no training exercise — this was the real thing. He was about to plant a bug on an actual target, not just a simulation.

With the nonchalance of a bored teenager, James passed families and couples, a planned meander toward the back of Stardt's temporary throne. As he neared, he calculated his steps and pace. It had to be just so...

He reached into the small canvas beach bag he was carrying, searching for something. His fingers wrapped around an object: a listening device. He started to pull it out. As his hand reached the bag opening, he fumbled, and the object fell back to the bottom.

Brilliant, he scolded himself. He went fishing again, finally extracting the item from his bag. He palmed it, casually letting his hand fall to his side. Now comes the tricky part... the actual plant.

He continued toward the vacant lounger. A particularly boisterous group of children ran past him, giving him the opportunity he needed. He faked a stumble as though they almost knocked him off his feet, then opened his hand to drop a perfect replica of a dog turd behind the German's chair. Acting annoyed that he almost stepped in the dropping, he scuffed a few grains of sand over it with his foot. The ersatz canine memento contained a listening device hidden inside something nobody would ever want to touch. Stardt was too engrossed in a copy of *Der Spiegel Magazine* to be aware of the activity in back of him.

James' heart hammered against his ribs, but his face betrayed none of the adrenaline coursing through him. When he reached the empty lounger, he congratulated himself for his skillful planting of the bug. He dropped the bag and a towel on the chair, ready to take up his post.

"Smooth move," a voice giggled from behind him.

James took in a quick breath, worried he wasn't as discrete as he thought. As he turned around, he saw two teenage girls with sun-kissed skin and sparkling eyes. One wore a bright polka-dot bikini while the other sported a vibrant turquoise one. Their giggling mixed in with the sound of crashing waves as they playfully nudged each other.

"For not stepping in it, she means," the shorter girl said.

"People should pick up after their dogs. Not cool." James' voice was tinged with what was close to a Scandinavian accent of some type. Part of the cover story Smith provided to him, most likely because of

James' blonde hair and blue eyes. He offered a lop-sided grin he hoped would disarm strangers — or potential threats. Although in this case, the former seemed more likely — but his training told him he could never be sure.

"You're not from around here, are you?" asked the taller of the two, her hair a cascade of sun-bleached curls.

"Is it that obvious?" James answered in mock surprise.

"Totally." The girl in the polka-dot bikini smiled and stepped closer. The other, with a dusting of freckles across her nose, nodded in eager agreement.

"Care to join us for a swim?" the taller girl tilted her head in the direction of the sparkling waves. The question was served with an inviting smile.

James couldn't help but enjoy being the object of the girl's flirtation, but he was also a bit embarrassed. Between the orphanage and his monk-like existence at the all-boys school, his experience with females his age was limited. Very limited. But, more importantly, he couldn't be distracted from his assignment. With a quick glance towards Stardt, he tried to figure a way to end the conversation gracefully. He slipped into the facade of a carefree teen. At least, like the ones he watched in the beach party movies.

"Not now, thanks. I want to catch some rays first." James peeled off his shirt. "We don't get sun like this in the north."

"Wow," breathed the freckled girl.

For a second, James didn't understand her reaction. He looked down at himself as though he spilled something. Then he got it... and grinned at his naivete. The girls giggled.

James had been the sole recruit at the training facility for over a month before anyone else arrived. He divided between the library and — thanks to Smith's not-so-subtle suggestion made in his dorm room — spending hours in the weight room. He hadn't aimed for a well-muscled physique for vanity. But he didn't mind the impressed glances the girls directed at him. He returned a modest half-shrug.

"Do you want our help to put on your suntan lotion?" the tall girl asked in a coy voice. Her friend nodded again.

"No, I'm good," James demurred.

"Your loss," the girls chimed together.

"You're right!" James flashed another grin. "Have a good swim. Maybe I'll catch up with you later." He winked. "Keep an eye out for sharks."

The girls ran off towards the water, their laughter hanging in the air like a promise.

James watched them go, the ghost of a smile lingering on his lips. Then, his blue eyes flickered back to Stardt, steeling once again with the resolve of a secret agent. As difficult as it was for him to believe sometimes, that was what he was: a secret agent. Not the average career for someone his age... or one that was announced to the world. He settled onto the lounger where he could keep an eye over both his concealed device and target.

The blazing sun beat down on the beach, causing the sand to sparkle like bits of glass. James' eyes remained fixed on the figure of Stardt. Not wanting to get sunburned on his first day in the field, James rummaged through his bag and retrieved a bottle of suntan lotion. He slathered the thick white cream all over his skin, regretting not taking up the girls' offer as he twisted to reach his back. It would have been easier — and much more fun.

Sighing, he settled himself to be comfortable, the warmth of the sun baking him. At least he wasn't sent to someplace like Siberia for his first job.

James gazed at the other people at the shore, practicing his observation skills by composing a report on their actions in his mind. Soon he grew bored watching them and wished he had brought something to read. The warm weather made him drowsy, and he struggled to keep his eyes open. He let out a long stretch, accompanied by a yawn. He wrote a mental note to himself: surveillance involves a great deal of boredom.

As Stardt lounged on the beach, a man in a crisp blue seersucker suit and a Panama hat headed his way. James went on alert as the other approached the German businessman.

The visitor who arrived at Stardt's lounger was a man in his late fifties. He stood tall and slender, with a lean build that radiated discipline. His facial features were chiseled and precise, like the cuts of a scalpel, and his black hair was streaked with strands of gray. There was a palpable sense of authority in his movements, but also a hint of subservience, the poor relation visiting the rich one.

Pretending to check the time, James raised his right wrist, although it wasn't a normal watch he wore. It was a Steineck ABC camera which at first glance resembled a wristwatch but held a lens that took photos on miniature circular film. He had practiced with the device; now to see if he got it correct.

James folded his hands together and rested them on his stomach, positioning the watch to capture Stardt's visitor. He used his left index finger to snap five quick shots. The man in the suit pulled the lounger to almost touching Stardt's and leaned in, as though not wanting to be overheard.

Without wasting a moment, James reached into his bag and retrieved what appeared to be a well-worn transistor radio. He plugged in the earpiece and placed it in his ear. Static crackled. He tuned the station dial until the voices transmitted from his bug came through, loud and clear.

"...mehr Informationen," Stardt's voice rumbled through the earpiece, tinged with impatience. "Bevor ich investiere."

"Es ist nicht so einfach," countered the man, his tone smooth like polished steel.

James's mind translated each German word effortlessly. He closed his eyes to help focus his attention on the conversation.

"Forty thousand is a lot of money — a fortune, one might say — yes, a fortune," Stardt said.

"Have you raised it?" The man in the suit sounded like a car huckster, desperate to close a deal. Looked like one, too.

Stardt sniffed his dismissal to this direct examination. "Of course. I have it with me here."

"Then what is your objection?" the man snapped. "You have already invested ten thousand."

"True, but that was a lesser amount than your newer request. Substantially less," said Stardt, shifting from the role of the prospect to the salesman. "First, doctor — forgive the caution. I am a businessman first, and I must have reasonable confidence that my investment will offer a profitable payment. I'm sure you understand."

"Herr Stardt, I assure you, the profits will be very pleasing."

"I am glad you are so confident," Stardt said dryly, "but the fact you need to return for additional capital raises concerns. It is necessary that I should know a little more about your remarkable scheme, for remarkable I am sure it is, before I contribute any more monies. For example, the legalities..."

"You are the one to be concerned about legalities!" the man fired back.

"I operate in areas that exist only within shades of gray, at the edge of the boundaries of the law," Stardt said, his voice smooth and calculated. "I must tread with care, for there are those who would be happy to see me fall. My actions are of interest to many, both inside and outside various governments."

Like the one listening to you now, James thought. He couldn't help but feel a surge of excitement. This was the world he trained for — the covert and perilous world that operated on the fringes and out of sight of polite society. Now it was his world, too.

"I will tell you this," the man wearing the suit said, appearing to choose his words with care. "My scheme falls into the narrow interpretation of the law as illegal. Do not mistake me, there is no danger to those who invest in ignorance. I will bear the full burden of responsibility."

"Of course, you understand that is incorrect. A shareholder in a 'scheme' cannot escape complete liability for the purposes to which the money is put," Stardt said abruptly. "You still do not provide enough specific information. I require more if you wish additional support from me."

There was a moment's pause as if the man was thinking things over. At last, he spoke. "As for my operation, I'm afraid I must ask you to invest in the dark. I can promise you that you will get your capital back a hundred times over. I realize that you have heard that sort of thing before..."

The German gave a knowing chuckle.

"... and that my suggestion has all the appearance of a confidence trick, except that I do not offer you even the substantial security of a gold brick," the man went on. "I may not require your money — I believe that I won't need to. On the other hand, I may. If it is to be of any use to me, it must be in my hands very soon — tomorrow, if possible."

There was such a long silence, James gave his radio a slight shake to see if it was still working.

"You wish me to further invest in a scheme in which you will not divulge any information, which you admit being illegal… in the narrow interpretation, as you say. This is a significant increase in my risk. Therefore, I require a fifty percent portion of all profits in order to contribute more capital."

"Fifty percent!" the man gasped. "Never!"

"That is what I'm offering you. I told you I operate on the fringes of legality, but I also have connections within many organizations, on both sides of the law. I give them valuable data in exchange for protection from their interference." Stardt's uncoiling threat was unmistakable. "Fifty percent is my price."

Cold water splashed over James. With a gasp, he jumped to his feet, dropping the radio, the earpiece coming loose. "What the —" James started to shout.

The two girls stood by the lounger, giggling. The one with freckles held a child's sand pail.

James didn't want to start a scene by yelling at the girls. What could he say? You interfered with my spy work? He couldn't afford to draw attention to himself. Forcing his anger at the interruption into a grin, he played along. But he still needed to get rid of them. He joined in the laughter, surprised at how natural he sounded. "Good one, good one."

"You wouldn't go to the ocean, so we brought the ocean to you." The tall girl laughed. "Where are you staying? Oh, I'm Penny."

"And I'm Kathy with a 'k'," the girl with the pail said.

"James." He gestured at the hotel. While doing so, he shot a glance toward Stardt and his visitor. Still present. Still talking... and he's still missing what they're saying. "I'm in there."

"So are we!" Penny exclaimed.

"With our parents," Kathy sullenly put in.

James smiled. "I'm solo."

"Maybe we all can go dancing," Penny hinted.

"All three of us?" He gave a wolfish grin.

"Natch!" Kathy said. "Unless you can't handle the two of us at once."

Kathy nudged Penny. "I bet he's afraid we'll wear him out."

"In your dreams, Kathy with a 'k'," James winked.

Penny spoke to Kathy. "Come on. We need to split." She smiled at him. "See you later. Um... room 423."

"451," Kathy said.

James grinned. "423 and 451. Got it. Ciao."

The girls finally ran off, and James turned his attention back to Stardt. His visitor's retreating form melded into the crowd, leaving the German alone again. James gave a growl of annoyance and resumed his seat. With a sigh, he reclined on the lounger, keeping his target within his field of vision. After a few minutes, James' instincts screamed that something was not right.

Stardt remained perfectly motionless, his unmoving bulk out of place to the bustling activity at the surrounding beach. James's keen eyes searched for any hint of movement from the businessman but found none. Unease began to creep over him. This was not part of the plan. It was a deviation that may have unforeseen consequences. James couldn't shake the nagging feeling that the game had just taken an unexpected and dangerous turn.

The Miami sun beat down, casting a glare that bounced off the ocean's surface and lent an almost surreal quality to the scene. The beachgoers around were oblivious, wrapped up in their own worlds of laughter and leisure.

With the thump of his pulse in his ears, James got to his feet. He gathered the transistor radio and earpiece, shoving them into his bag, followed by his shirt. Hoisting the sack, he tread over the hot sand, trying to move with the ease of someone accustomed to being unnoticed. As he neared Stardt, a sudden hush seemed to fall over the area — an unseen cloud dimming the vibrant scene.

Stardt was slumped on the lounger as if in a deep sleep, his mouth slightly open. But the chilling absence of life raised the hairs on the back of James' neck. His gaze dropped. The magazine lay on the businessman's stomach, and underneath the pages, a knife handle protruding from the man's side. The dripping blood formed a dark stain on the pristine sand.

James' heart hammered against his ribs, a staccato rhythm mirrored by the waves crashing onto the shore. He scanned the vicinity. No one appeared to have noticed the grim scene just yet. His training took control, almost automatically. This was a complication. His assignment certainly didn't include the possibility of the target's murder.

Stepping back, James blended once more into the crowd, his every move calculated to appear normal while his brain worked furiously. It was time to disappear into the shadows, to become a ghost among the living. He also had some work to do, but fast. His foot pushed the phony dog turd deep into the sand, then he headed for the hotel.

Chapter Two

J AMES STROLLED THROUGH THE hotel lobby on the way to his room. He wanted to rush, but that would call attention to himself. Not the thing to do if somebody had spotted him next to Stardt's body.

"Mr. Vagus," the bell captain called out. Marty was short, slight, and wore his bellhop outfit like a military uniform. "Did you enjoy your time on the beach?"

"Quite memorable, Marty," James responded with a smile. The sizeable tip James had given worked. Marty could be a source of needed information.

James made his way down a lengthy corridor, the sound of his steps swallowed by the plush carpet. The murder of Stardt added an unexpected twist to James' first assignment, pushing it out of the "routine" column. Based on what he overheard, James was convinced that the man in the seersucker suit was responsible for Stardt's death. It seemed they were business partners, but something had caused their relationship to come to a sudden, and violent, end. James had captured photos of this enigmatic figure… assuming he had properly operated the camera.

MIS-X had booked him into a first-floor room next to Stardt's, with a connecting door between them. That permitted James to maintain his surveillance easily. As he passed Stardt's door, an unexpected sound made him freeze in his tracks. He placed his ear to the door.

Someone was inside the room, and it couldn't be the fat German businessman unless he rose from the dead. Unlocking his door as quietly as he could, he slipped into his own room. He closed the drapes, blocking the beautiful first-floor view of the ocean — as well as anybody spying on him while he was doing the same on somebody else.

James searched through the equipment in his luggage and pulled out a fiberscope. The device had a pistol-grip handle, with a long fiber-optic cable attached to it, measuring 48 long. The hotel was built in the 1920s and still featured old-fashioned locks. By looking through the tiny viewfinder of the instrument, he could peer into Stardt's room through the keyhole of the connecting door. It would give him an opportunity to catch a glimpse of whoever was paying the unauthorized visit. James positioned himself on his knees in front of the keyhole and carefully threaded the end of the cable through it. He pressed his eye to the viewer.

Darkness shrouded the room beyond, the blinds also drawn tight against the sun's probing rays. Despite the dim conditions, James made out the figure of a man rifling through the contents of the room. He was not being messy but was going through drawers and baggage with great care, making sure nothing appeared disturbed.

James squinted, trying to make out the man's features. In the dim light, he couldn't, but the man was wearing a seersucker suit. It could be the same man who had visited Stardt earlier on the beach. And, presumably, the man who knifed him.... unless seersucker suits were the "in" fashion this season for burglars.

An abrupt, piercing scream shattered the afternoon calm, making its way from the outdoors to James's ears. Someone had obviously discovered Stardt's lifeless body.

Through the fiberscope, James watched as the intruder suddenly paused in his search, clearly having heard the scream as well. He seemed to weigh his options for a moment before continuing with his task. He tossed one bag on the bed, opened it, and ran his fingers around the inside lining. With a soft chuckle, the man pulled out a stack of bills and pocketed the cash, replacing the suitcase where he found it. Making his way to the window, he slipped out and disappeared from view.

"Well, he got his investment after all," James said to himself. Although part of him wanted to follow the murderer, he decided it would be better for him to take something out of Stardt's room as well. The bugs he planted earlier would cause questions if discovered by the police. Their presence was now a liability, possibly revealing the government's interest in Stardt and complicating matters.

He returned the fiberscope to his luggage, removing a pair of gloves and something like a pocket knife. Instead of blades, it held a selection of lock-picking tools. With deft fingers, James unlocked the door for the second time today. As the door clicked open, he hesitated for just a moment, glancing back at his room as if expecting somebody to be following him. Slipping on the gloves, he stepped into the dimly lit room Stardt had occupied... until recently.

The lingering scent of cigar smoke, Cuban most likely, hung heavy in the air, a reminder of Stardt's preference for indulgence haunting the space. James moved to a nightstand by the bed. He reached behind, his fingers locating the bug he had planted earlier. He pulled it off and went to the desk. Off came the hidden microphone he'd stuck under it. His gaze fell upon the desktop. James hadn't paid attention to it earlier when he was intent on placing the bugs.

Notes and commodity price data lay scattered across the surface. Today's *Wall Street Journal*, open to the charts for corn and wheat, rested next to the papers. Now James' instincts told him that something was off. Stardt's dossier never mentioned any business interest in crop prices.

As he leaned down to investigate any further, the sound of voices drifted in from the hallway outside. They grew louder with each passing second.

"Nothing like this has ever happened at the Ocean View Resort before," a voice worried. Most likely the hotel manager. "I don't want anything to get in the newspapers."

"Murder always gets in the papers," came a gruff response. James guessed that somebody was from the police.

"Oh, dear, oh dear." James could almost see the manager wringing his hands.

They would be at the door at any moment. James couldn't afford to be caught in there; it would certainly lead to awkward questions. He darted back to his own room.

"Is this his?" the detective asked.

James closed the door and braced himself against it, his heart hammering in his chest. But with a surge of panic, he realized he had forgotten to lock the door. Frantically searching for the pocketknife, he found and grabbed it. His hands shook as he fumbled with the picks, just as the sound of jingling keys echoed from the hallway. He secured the door just as the one to Stardt's room opened. James held his breath.

"Has anybody been in here?" the detective went on. "Maid?"

"Housekeeping attends to these rooms in the morning," the hotel manager replied.

The detective gave an annoyed huff. "Where does this door go?"

"It leads to the adjoining room, but it's locked. Only the staff have a key."

The knob of the communicating door rattled.

"Seal this room," the detective ordered. "Nobody is to come in here. I'll send the lab boys over."

"Of course."

The door to Stardt's room closed, the key clicking in the lock.

James exhaled, paced across the plush carpet of his room, and sat on the bed. He dropped the bugs and pocketknife next to him.

"Alright, now what?" James said to himself, removing the gloves and slapping them down on the bedspread as he thought about what he should do next. Report in and ask? The training emphasized the agent being autonomous in the field… and he didn't want to announce the failure of his initial mission on the first day to Smith. After a few moments, he decided to lie low and stick to the original plan. He may pick up more useful information, and, if he didn't, all Smith could do would be to scream about a few extra days' hotel charges.

First, there was the camera to deal with. He went to the dresser, poked around the change he'd put in the ashtray, and picked up a fifty-cent piece. It popped open after he pressed at a particular spot, revealing a hollow interior. Unstrapping the watch, he took it and the coin halves into the bathroom, closing the door. He left the light off.

James deftly opened the camera's sleek casing by touch. He carefully removed the negative, ensuring not to damage the delicate circle. Holding the hollowed-out half-dollar in his other hand, he gingerly placed the film inside and snapped the top section on with a reassuring click.

With the photos safely stashed away, James allowed himself a moment of rest. He put away all his equipment before he reclined on the bed, his head swimming with questions and partially formed ideas. Had Stardt been involved in something far bigger than what was initially suspected? And where did the sudden influx of cash Stardt's visitor needed fit into all of this? And what about corn prices? How did they figure in? Or did they?

Although the thoughts were intriguing, James figured they weren't his concern — yet. Since the object of his surveillance mission would soon occupy a slab at the county morgue, he might as well slot in some vacation before receiving his new instructions.

Rolling off the bed, he changed into a light blue polo shirt, gray slacks, and black shoes. He grinned as he caught sight of his reflection in the mirror, frankly admiring himself. After wearing charity and cast-off clothes all his life, it was great to walk into a store and buy his own stylish outfits. Especially now MIS-X was providing a clothing allowance.

Slipping the hollow coin into his pocket, he grabbed his wallet and headed to the lobby. The room buzzed with hushed conversations, the news of Stardt's murder apparently having spread like wildfire. The guests huddled in groups, talking while the staff endeavored to be above it all, acting as if nothing unusual had happened. An elderly man, his face flushed with excitement, came up to James. "Terrible business, isn't it?"

"Very." James forced a suitable grim expression. "You never expect something like this to happen when you're on vacation."

"Indeed, young man. Indeed." The gentleman nodded. He shuffled away to join another group of people. "Terrible business, isn't it?"

Crossing the lobby with purpose, James approached the rental car counter where a bored-looking woman sat, filing papers.

"Good afternoon," James said. "My name is James Vagus. I'm here to pick up a vehicle rented for me by Mr. Smith."

"Driver's license, please," the agent said, holding out one hand.

James handed his over, watching as the woman's eyes flicked over it before a frown creased her brow. "I'm sorry, sir, we don't rent vehicles to people under 21 years of age."

"Could you please check your records again?" James kept his tone even and patient. He knew Smith would have sorted this out in advance.

With an annoyed sigh, she flipped through her forms for a moment. Her expression shifted to surprise. "My apologies, Mr. Vagus. I see you have an open-ended, paid-for rental. It's ready for you." She opened a drawer and pulled on some keys. She handed them to him with a smile. "It's in space ten. Go out the door and turn right. Oh, and here's your contract."

"Thank you." James retrieved his license, the paperwork, and the keys.

Stepping outside in the bright Miami sun, he slipped on his sunglasses. He walked down the row of cars, whistling and tossing the keys in the air with his hand. That all stopped when he reached the space, occupied by the most boring four-door beige sedan he could imagine. It was the kind of car that mix into any environment with ease — perfect for undercover work, but that's about all that could be said about it.

"Not exactly James Bond's Aston Martin," James said ruefully, climbing into the driver's seat and adjusting the mirrors. He pulled out of the lot, intending simply to drive around Miami for a while. But Penny and Kathy came to mind. Since his mission was on hold with nobody living to put under surveillance, perhaps he could afford one evening of fun.

Steering back toward the Ocean View, he parked and went back to the lobby. After hesitating for a second, nervous, he penned a note for both the girls on hotel stationery. Slipping the papers into envelopes, he approached the front desk.

"Could you please put these in the box for 423?" James handed the envelopes to the clerk.

The clerk took them. "Of course, sir."

"Thank you." James turned away. "Who knows?" he thought as he headed back to the car.

***

James wandered into the lobby, checking his watch. Again. Five minutes. In five minutes, he'll find out if he'd been stood up, and the girls were in their rooms, laughing at his naivety or not. His eyes scanned the area as he once more tightened his tie unnecessarily.

While he anxiously waited for Penny and Kathy to arrive, he couldn't help but feel a knot of nerves in his stomach. This was not just any date — it was a date with not one, but two girls. He had never done anything like this before, and his past few dates never led to second ones. The image of suave movie star Cary Grant flashed through his mind. That's who he'd be tonight: charming and sophisticated, like the silver screen icon. He would play the part of Cary Grant.

The sound of footsteps and feminine laughter drew his attention, and he straightened up to see Penny and Kathy approaching, their eyes bright with excitement.

"Hey, there you are!" Penny came up to him, waving a hand in greeting. "We were wondering if those notes were jokes."

"Never." James took Penny's hand and pressed a light kiss to her knuckles. After Smith gave James his Nordic cover story, he took a crash course in Swedish. Time to see if it stuck. "Jag skulle aldrig skämta med två vackra damer."

"Norwegian?" Kathy asked.

"Swedish," James also kissed her hand. "I'm from Stockholm, remember? I said, 'I would never joke with two beautiful ladies.'"

"That sounds more romantic than in French!" Kathy said.

"Je ne dirais pas ça," James grinned.

The girls giggled.

"How many languages do you speak?" Penny gushed.

"I'm fluent in Spanish, French, German, and Mandarin," James listed.

"Aren't you forgetting one?" Kathy asked.

"I am?"

"English," Kathy teased.

James flushed in embarrassment at the omission. "Yes, of course. English."

"You sound as if you spoke it your entire life. You don't even have an accent," Kathy said.

Because I forgot to use one, James thought, irritated at himself for another oversight. "Thank you." Time to move the subject of languages before he made another mistake. "I am a business student at Stockholm University."

"We're from Nebraska," Penny said.

"And we have to go back tomorrow," Kathy added in a morose tone.

"Then I promise you, it'll be an evening to remember." James clicked his heels together and gave a slight bow.

"Such a gentleman," Kathy said, a playful smile tugging at the corners of her lips. "So, where are we headed tonight?"

"The bell captain recommended The Beachcomber," James offered an arm to either girl. The trio started for the parking lot.

"Can you believe what happened?" Kathy said, her eyes wide with a mixture of excitement and horror. "A real-life murder, right here at our hotel!"

"It's wild," Penny said. "I've never been this close to a murder investigation before."

"Neither have I," James said smoothly, keeping his expression neutral.

"Who do you think did it?" Kathy asked, leaning in closer to James. "The police must have some suspects by now, right?"

James spoke in a low, conspiratorial voice, "I think the butler did it." The girls laughed, Penny slapping James on the arm. "But I'm sure the authorities will catch the guilty party soon."

"Let's just hope we're not next," Penny chimed in with a nervous chuckle.

The group reached the car. James opened the passenger door. "I propose no more talk about murder tonight. I want to know all about Nebraska."

"That won't take long," Kathy said as she climbed into the sedan.

The night ahead would require skill for James to maintain his assumed identity, a type of practical exam. He hoped he had enough information on Stockholm to satisfy any questions the girls had. But for now, as he got into the driver's seat, he allowed himself to enjoy the moment. He would embrace the role of the charming, suave spy. Even if he had to drive a boring, beige four-door sedan.

At breakfast the next morning, James couldn't help but smile as he relived his outing last night. After his initial rough start with the languages he spoke, he had maintained his cover of a Swedish business student with ease, weaving elaborate stories, creating friends and a past. Hiding behind this false identity, James was more relaxed on a date than he ever had been before when he was, well, himself. He was disappointed, however, to discover his karate training had done little to improve his dancing skills.

James put down his coffee as he stared at the news article on Stardt's murder. It brought him back to his job at hand. Today, he was scheduled to meet his contact to pass on whatever information he had uncovered. And did he have some. Finishing breakfast, he slipped the newspaper into his jacket pocket and headed out to Flagler Street, Miami's busy shopping hub.

The bustling avenue was alive with the constant movement of people and vehicles. Three and four-story buildings lined either side, each adorned with vibrant storefronts and colorful signs. Every few blocks, taller offices like the Biscayne Building and New Florida National Bank rose into the sky, standing out over the sea of smaller structures. Movie theaters were sprinkled among the shops, their bright marquees enticing passersby with promises of entertainment in air-conditioned darkness. James strolled down the sidewalk, stopping in front of the McCrorys store. He checked his watch, then he heard a voice in back of him.

"Hey mister, got some change to spare?"

Right on time. James pivoted to face a disheveled stranger who was about his age and was slightly shorter. The young man's hand was stretched out towards him, but his eyes remained hidden by dark sunglasses. Long, straight black hair hung down to his shoulders, framing a handsome face. He had olive skin, a chiseled jawline, high cheekbones, and a straight nose. Behind those shades, James knew there were a pair of deep brown eyes that exuded both tranquility and alertness.

The beachcomber's name was Dakota Walker. Smith had teamed him and James together during training, and they quickly merged into one entity. The two seemed to share some kind of connection, always knowing what the other was thinking or about to do. Even so, not a flicker of recognition crossed either face.

"You beach bums ought to get jobs, instead of sponging off the rest of us," James said in an irritated voice.

"Hey man, take it easy. No need to stress." The beachcomber raised his hands in a calming gesture. "Negativity's like a bad tide, gotta let it wash away, man, wash away."

"Here." The sun glinted off the half-dollar as he flipped it to Dakota. His partner snatched the coin in midair with a fluid, precise movement. James pulled out the newspaper from his jacket and handed it over as well. "Take a look at it." He tapped on the article about Stardt's murder. "You may find something interesting... like help wanted ads."

"Peace, love, and sandy toes, dude." Dakota flashed the peace sign.

Dakota turned and left, mingling into the crowds of Flagler Street before he disappeared. James allowed himself a fleeting smile. Peace, love, and sandy toes?

James drove back to the hotel. Entering the lobby, a man caught his attention: it was the same one who had visited Stardt on the beach and most likely took the money from the room. He was speaking to an attractive younger woman, who was perhaps in her late twenties. She was tall, lithe, with blonde hair cascading to her shoulders. Despite her poise and elegance, she projected an undercurrent of danger — a Venus Flytrap waiting to snatch any nearby insect daring to fly too close.

"The old saying must be true," he said to himself. "Criminals do return to the scene of their crime."

James passed them and walked to a nearby wall map. A handy potted palm separated him from the two. Hiding behind a potted palm to spy... how cliché, he thought as he moved into position.

"... need more investors," the man was saying to the woman, "At present, I find myself with insufficient capital to go forward. It is my intention to secure what I require."

The woman gestured to the resort. Her voice was smokey. "There are sure to be plenty of marks here.

The wealthy gather here like animals at the watering hole at sundown."

"Apparently," the man said with acid tones. "I should get the shipment Wednesday. I will need you to make a delivery on Thursday."

The woman nodded in response and headed towards the registration desk, while the man made his way to the exit. James hurried over to the counter and stood beside her. They exchanged cordial smiles as they waited for the clerk to finish his phone call.

James gestured for the woman to go first when the clerk approached them.

"Room 306, please," she said.

"Of course, Miss Glaum." The clerk gave her the key. After another polite smile to James, her eyes appraising him, the woman sauntered away.

"115, Mr. Vagus?" the clerk asked.

"Please."

The clerk leaned forward slightly and spoke in a low voice. "You haven't been disturbed by... the incident, have you, Mr. Vagus? After all, your room is..."

James shook his head. "No, I haven't been inconvenienced at all. I've hardly noticed."

The clerk returned a relieved expression as he handed over his key. James took it and walked toward the hallway, but detoured to the bell desk.

"Marty," he asked the bell captain, "do you know who Miss Glaum is?"

Marty grinned. "Indeed I do, sir. Who could miss her?"

James discretely slipped a twenty-dollar bill across the desk. "Can you find out how long her stay is?"

Marty winked as he pocketed the cash. "Of course, Mr. Vagus."

Returning a knowing grin, James continued for his room. Miss Glaum's relationship with Stardt's visitor needed more investigation.

Chapter Three

P ALM FRONDS WHISPERED IN the sea breeze as James' sneakers crunched over the gravel path of Crandon Park. The morning sun cast a golden sheen over Biscayne Bay, but James was not here to bask in the Miami heat or scenic views. He scanned the area and smiled when he located Dakota seated under a palm tree, facing the water.

Growing up at the orphanage, James learned not to get too attached to anyone. He had made friends with the other kids, only to see them get adopted and leave while he remained behind. Eventually, he decided it was easier to keep everyone at a distance, a shield from the pain of losing someone again. He couldn't help but wonder if Dakota saw him in the same way. Like James, the Cherokee teen kept his past hidden and refused to discuss it... politely, but firmly. James knew nothing about Dakota's history before he showed up for training. Perhaps Dakota too had built walls around himself for similar reasons to James.

"Morning," James said, taking a seat by his partner. "Next time, we need to be more specific about the meeting place. Something like 'third palm tree from the right.' This park is huge."

Dakota's nod was curt. "That was very selfish of you, you know."

James looked at Dakota, puzzled. "What? You sound like I ate the only chocolate doughnut."

"Escorting those young ladies to The Beachcomber last night." Dakota held up two fingers. "A pair of them. By yourself."

"How did you know that?" James asked in amazement.

"I saw you."

"You tailed me?"

Dakota gave a half smile and a shrug. "You never know when you'll need backup."

"How thoughtful," James said. "Where were you? I didn't spot you."

"I didn't intend for you to," Dakota answered.

James chuckled. "I forget. You move like a cat and can see in the dark."

Dakota leaned back against the palm tree. "Meow, baby."

"Jealous?" James nudged Dakota.

"You bet your sweet bippy I am!" Dakota returned a grin.

"Do you have any information for me or are you going to complain all day?" James flashed a sugary smile.

Dakota groaned. He switched to Cherokee. "Information."

After finding out about James' talent for languages when training began, Dakota proposed the idea of teaching him Cherokee. Without hesitation, James agreed, demanding Dakota only speak it to him during their free time. Despite the complexity of the language — it was about as hard to him as Mandarin — he managed to learn enough to have conversations with Dakota, giving the pair a handy, private code.

"Stardt's visitor, the one in the photos you took, is one Dr. Victor van Heerden," Dakota said.

"Medical?"

Dakota nodded. His voice was low and even. "He's a Dutch citizen, but born in Germany. When he immigrated to the Netherlands, he changed his name from 'von' to 'van'. But that's the least interesting part of his resume."

James leaned in, his senses on high alert.

"During the war, there was talk about him being friendly, shall we say, with the Nazis, especially when they occupied the country." Dakota's impassive face did little to hide the gravity of his words. "There were rumors of his collaboration at the Westerbork concentration camp."

"Medical experimentation?" James' stomach turned even as he asked.

Dakota nodded grimly.

"Anything proven?"

"No war crimes charge. Smoke without fire, officially. But we both know where there's smoke..." Out of training, Dakota's voice trailed off as a young couple walked by, holding hands. He and James discretely watched the pair until they were out of earshot.

"Sometimes the fire's been carefully put out," James finished the thought. "Like with those Nazi rocket scientists we brought over here after the war."

Dakota picked up where he had left off. "As I said, van Heerden was never charged with war crimes and completed the de-Nazification process successfully. He then didn't just vanish into the background. Just the opposite, in fact. He's been busy. The doctor lived down criticism, lived down suspicion, and established a thriving medical practice. He owned the largest flat in a beautiful building in Amsterdam, with one room set up as a laboratory. His passion for research, apparently, stayed with him."

"Any idea on type?"

Dakota shrugged. "Unknown. Then a few years ago, he simply dropped out of sight."

"It sounds like he's back in it."

"You got it. In Amsterdam, he's been observed making several visits to the Soviet, Polish, East German, Czechoslovakian and Hungarian embassies," Dakota said. "There are also whispers of him trying to entice investors into a scheme he's dreamed up."

"Probably the reason he visited those embassies." James stretched and made himself more comfortable against the palm trunk. "To whip up some money... or try to."

"That is possible. And the selection of which countries is interesting. All Communist governments. So whatever van Heerden's idea is, it can't be any good for the West."

James nodded. "Any scoop about what the scheme is all about?"

Dakota shook his head. "He sold his place in Amsterdam and moved into a small hotel there. He's visiting here on a tourist visa."

"Selling his flat got him some cash, but obviously he needs more. That's what he was trying to do with Stardt, to get him to invest additional money in something. It wasn't clear what that something was," James said. "Except Stardt became too greedy about the proceeds. Even threatened blackmail if he didn't get the cut he demanded."

"And that got him killed?"

"Seems like the most logical answer." James shaded his eyes and watched a sailboat skim across the water.

Dakota's dry sense of humor was absent now. "We need to tread carefully around van Heerden."

"What about Smith? What did he say about Stardt's killing?" James asked after a pause. He wondered if somehow he would be blamed.

"It annoyed him," Dakota answered, "like he misplaced his car keys."

James sighed. "I guess that ends our first assignment. I'll go to the police and tell them what I know."

Dakota cut him off. "No, Smith doesn't want us involved in the local murder investigation at all."

"Then what?" James looked at Dakota, puzzled.

"Our orders are to remain here and find out what van Heerden is up to," Dakota said. "Smith says to use our judgment on how to proceed."

"So we're on our own." James gazed over the blue waters of the bay.

"Could be worse," Dakota said, with the hint of a dry laugh. "He could've given us an order that would get us killed."

"How comforting," James muttered, a half-smirk twisting his lips. "So instead, he throws us into the deep end to see if we can swim."

Dakota tapped James on the shoulder. When James looked, Dakota locked his eyes on him. "I don't plan to drown."

James returned the gaze with equal intensity. "Neither do I."

The two were quiet for a moment. James sat back, processing the information, his mind piecing together a mosaic from the bits of data he had. It was a puzzle, with pieces scattered across history and continents, perhaps involving old war secrets and new alliances. And he and Dakota were going to put it into one picture. James shifted, feeling the grainy texture of the bench beneath him. Then he remembered the encounter in the lobby.

"Alright, let me lay this on you," James began, leaning forward as if the sea breeze could carry away their words, "Van Heerden returned to the hotel yesterday, and spoke to another guest." Dakota's interest sharpened, the subtle tilt of his head posing an unspoken question.

"It was a Miss Glaum," James clarified. "The two were like a pair of rattlesnakes poised to strike."

"Did they exchange anything?" Dakota asked.

"Nothing physical," James admitted, pulling the image back into his mind. "And this Miss Glaum... she seemed almost deferential to him."

"Deferential?"

"Exactly. Like an employee to an employer." James said.

"So the fact she is staying at the same hotel as Stardt isn't a coincidence," Dakota said.

"It must not be," James agreed.

Dakota said, "Van Heerden's history with the Nazis, his attempted contacts with the Eastern Bloc, this investor plan of his — it's a puzzle with too many missing pieces." He thought for a moment. "His returning to the hotel suggests he doesn't think he was spotted talking to Stardt... that he's in the clear."

"True," James nodded, "or he's desperate."

"For..."

"Money. From what I overheard, part of Miss Glaum's job is to line up more investors. 'Marks', she called them. The hotel is loaded with them, she believes." James glanced around, noting the sun glinting off the waves of the bay, the way the light fractured, a dance of shadows and sunspots that danced in front of him. The park was peaceful, different from the upset of uncertainty churning inside him. "Van Heerden is returning to the hotel on Saturday. He wants Miss Glaum to make a delivery."

"Of what?"

James shrugged. "Don't have a clue."

"Which is why we follow them," Dakota said, decisive. "This Miss Glaum and van Heerden — they're keys to unlocking this. We shadow them, find out what they're up to."

"Tail them separately or together." It was less a question than a confirmation of a plan.

"There's two of them and two of us. Separately. Cover more ground that way," Dakota suggested, his eyes narrowing as he considered their options. "We need to know where they go, who they meet. Every detail could be the one that matters."

"Agreed," James said. "Who gets who?"

Dakota pulled a half-dollar from his pocket. "Call it." He flicked a silver coin high into the air where it caught the morning light, spinning with a glint before descending into his waiting palm. He covered it.

"Heads!" James called out, his gaze fixed on Dakota's closed hand.

"Guess today isn't your lucky day," Dakota lifted his hand. The coin rested tails up. "I'll take Miss Glaum. To make up for last night."

"I ought to double-check that. See if it's legit." James reached for the coin.

"Don't you trust me?" Dakota said in mock hurt, pocketing the half-dollar with a swift motion.

"No."

"You just gotta take my word for it," Dakota said.

James grinned. "Stay sharp."

"Always am," Dakota said, the barest nod sealing their plan.

"Whatever they're up to, I have a feeling it's bigger than we first thought. And I have a hunch van Heerden's scheme is at the heart of it." James stood and headed back to his car.

The game had begun, and the chase was on. And he was determined neither he nor Dakota would rest until they unraveled the tangled web of secrets that Victor van Heerden had woven. The weight of their mission settled upon his shoulders like a cloak. The two had trained for this moment, but was it enough? Yet, they had no choice but to put their faith in their training and each other. It was a dangerous match they were playing.

***

Dakota lounged on a bench positioned alongside the Ocean View Hotel's sidewalk the next day as he waited for James' signal. He plugged in an earpiece from his transistor radio and focused on the vast Atlantic in front of him through his sunglasses. He craved a swim, but he wasn't sure when Miss Glaum and van Heerden would meet. Suddenly, James' voice, transmitted through the small body microphone he wore, sounded distorted and faint in Dakota's ear.

"She's exiting the lobby now. Blonde hair, wearing a blue dress." James crackled out.

Dakota stood, removing the earpiece as he headed to his motorcycle. Storing the radio in one saddlebag, he straddled the bike. His sharp vision quickly picked up his quarry. He nodded in approval.

A tall, slender man dressed in a brown suit approached Miss Glaum. Dakota assumed his name was van Heerden. He seemed impatient and stood with a rigid posture. The woman calmly walked towards him, her steps deliberate and giving no indication of her thoughts. The two figures met, and van Heerden handed over a plain salesman's case to Miss Glaum with a swift, rehearsed movement. She took the case firmly in her hand without exchanging any words or lingering glances. It was a routine transaction that lacked any warmth or emotion.

With the case now in her possession, she turned on her heel and strode confidently towards a white convertible, gleaming under the bright Miami sun. Out of the corner of his eye, Dakota spotted James as he stepped out of the lobby and pretended to check his watch near the entrance doors.

Dakota started his motorcycle, the roar of the engine drowning out everything else. His entire being became consumed by the task at hand, his senses honed. As Miss Glaum's car pulled away from the curb, Dakota merged into traffic like a cat stalking a bird as he transferred his skills at tracking from the forest to the street. He blended in completely, his presence as subtle as a shadow gliding over the water.

The dance of surveillance began, with Dakota never taking his eyes off the convertible. He sometimes left a vehicle between them. Other times he passed Miss Glaum and remained in front, letting her then pass him. Each turn and stop occurred with precision, the rumble of his motorcycle a throbbing soundtrack to the pursuit. Like a hawk fixated on its target, Dakota tracked each change in direction, every stop and go, his determination unbreakable. He wasn't planning out each maneuver. They simply happened... automatic, instinctual, feral.

The Miami heat clung to Dakota's skin like a second layer as the convertible turned on NW 40th Street, an industrial area of the city. He guided his bike past bland, characterless warehouses and small factories. Ahead, the white car slowed, easing to a stop outside a nondescript building. Dakota gunned his bike, glancing at the address as he zoomed by the car. As he waited at a stop sign, he checked his side mirror.

Miss Glaum climbed out, carrying the salesman's case like she was selling cosmetics door-to-door.

Dakota took a right turn and parked his bike. He walked to the corner and observed as she made her way toward a single steel door that broke the plain wall. The door opened slightly, just enough for her to enter. Dakota quickly moved down the street to the warehouse. Turning down an alleyway that ran next to the building, he circled to an asphalt parking lot in the back. Tall windows, running from a third of the way up to the roof, filled the rear wall. Scanning them, Dakota spotted one that didn't look completely closed.

He jogged to it, slipping his fingers between the casement and the frame. He tugged. Unlatched. It was an awning-type window, and he pulled it open. With the grace of a puma, Dakota hoisted himself through the aperture, landing lightly on a concrete floor layered with dirt.

The warehouse interior sprawled out before him. The light filtering in through the high windows revealed a barren area, void of any life or movement. Only a few scattered items broke up the expanse: a metal dolly, its wheels caked with dust, and a couple of empty crates stacked haphazardly against the wall. Along one side of the room, cables hung down from rusted circuit boxes, remnants of long-gone machines that once hummed with life. It was a hollow, eerie place, forgotten by time and purpose.

At one end of the space, a door stood open. The hum of voices and the sound of bubbling liquids escaped into the air. Dakota padded forward, each step measured and soundless, the dry scent of dust and disuse filling his nostrils. He pressed himself against the wall by the doorway.

"Is that all you require, Bridgers?" Miss Glaum said.

Something sounding like the tinkling of milk bottles came from the room.

"Yeah," Bridgers said. There was a moment's quiet, then he continued, his voice heavy with sarcasm. He gestured to the surroundings. "Rather a comedown for one of the top analytical chemists that the university ever turned out, eh?"

Miss Glaum sighed. "Are you going to go through that again? You're being well paid for your work."

"But not to ask questions, is that it? Just shut up and follow orders. Sounds like something from a few years ago." Bridgers lowered his voice. "Say, you're van Heerden's girl — what is his game?"

"What is — ?" Miss Glaum started.

"What is his game? What is it all about? I've tried to pump Gregory and Milsom, but they're mysterious," Bridgers said in an urgent tone. "What is going on? Why is he sending men to America, Canada, Australia, and India? Come along and be a pal! Tell me! I've seen his desk. I know all about it. Tickets and itineraries. You don't fool me!" The last words came almost at a hiss. "Why is he employing the crooks and the throw-outs of science? Perrilli, Maxon, Boyd, Heyler — and me? If the game's square, why doesn't he take the new graduates from the schools?"

"I'm sure I don't know," Miss Glaum fired back. "And I'm not his 'girl'. I just work for him like everybody else."

Bridger's response was a mocking laugh.

The door opened suddenly. Dakota shrank into the shadows of the corner. Miss Glaum stepped out, holding the sample case. She was followed by a man Dakota assumed was Bridgers — a tall, skinny, pale man with salt and pepper hair and shallow cheeks. He smacked his lips and pulled the little tortoise-shell box of his lab coat. He opened the lid, revealing a white powder. "Are you sure? Try a sniff — and all your troubles will go — phutt!"

Miss Glaum glared at Bridgers. "That stuff is the reason you're a throw-out. And why you work and not ask questions."

A chortle came from Bridgers as he slipped the container back into his pocket. "You're the loser, honey. You'll never find heaven on earth!"

After throwing a disgusted look toward Bridgers, Miss Glaum walked out of the warehouse. Bridgers returned to the office, leaving the door ajar.

Dakota remained hidden in the shadows, holding his breath and staying as silent as a ghost. He waited for Hilda's footsteps to fade away completely before stepping forward. With tense muscles, he inched closer to the door and peered through the narrow gap between it and the frame.

The room that was once an office now served as a chemical lab, with two long tables cluttered with glassware, vials, and precision instruments. In the corner, Bridgers dressed himself in white protective overalls. Singing softly, he donned a pair of green-glass goggles, giving him an otherworldly appearance. The chemist approached a table and picked up a flask, holding it up in front of him and swirling its contents.

Shifting his position slightly, Dakota attempted to get a better view of the laboratory. A sudden force blindsided him, a crushing blow to the back of his head. Red-hot pain exploded across his senses, the world tilting off-kilter. Dakota's body folded beneath the weight of darkness as it clawed its way into his consciousness. The floor came up to meet him.

Chapter Four

J AMES WATCHED AS DAKOTA sped by on his motorcycle, then shifted his attention to van Heerden. The doctor climbed into a blue sedan. Hurrying to his rental, James picked up van Heerden as he pulled out of the hotel parking lot.

The car's engine hummed a steady note as James shadowed van Heerden through the Miami streets. He kept his distance, two car lengths behind, mixing in with the sparse traffic, scanning the road ahead and the rearview mirror with mechanical precision.

Van Heerden turned onto a quiet residential street, lined with neat rows of small, cozy houses on large lots. He pulled into the driveway of a bungalow on the corner; its single-story structure painted a crisp white and topped with a flat roof. The aluminum awning-style windows glinted in the afternoon sunlight, and colorful tropical plants edged the foundation. Van Heerden disappeared inside the structure.

James couldn't help but give a half-smile when he saw the house next door had a bright red "For Sale" sign planted in its yard. Perfect. He parked in front.

With a small leather travel pouch in one hand and the rental car contract in the other, James climbed out of the driver's seat. He glanced down at the paper as if it contained vital information about the property, then directed his gaze to the house for sale. He strolled along the side, inspecting every inch of the home as if he were a seasoned real estate agent. When he reached the back, he looked around to ensure he remained unseen.

The backyard of the bungalow van Heerden occupied was well planted, obscuring it from the neighbors. James hopped over the low brick wall separating the properties and sprinted to the white house. Hiding behind a big, flowering oleander, he opened the leather pouch and retrieved the Motel Kit — a compact assembly of espionage essentials. He put on the stethoscopic earphones and plugged them into the amplifier unit. Attaching the transducer, he placed the sensitive microphone on the stucco. The device picked up vibrations from the other side of the wall, sending the sounds to James' earphones.

The buzz of a phone conversation trickled into his ear. James closed his eyes, letting his trained mind sharpen the muffled words into clarity. He could hear van Heerden's voice now, tinged with frustration and urgency.

"I have offered my scheme to sympathetic governments." His voice trembled with passion. "I glory in a stateless and egalitarian society... obtained through might if necessary. I believe it better that the old civilization be stamped into the mud of oblivion... the licentious French, the mercenary English, the dollar-hunting Yankees — But the powers I contact fear touching my plan. Scared!"

Through the earpiece, the timbre of van Heerden's speech escalated into a crescendo of disgruntlement, before falling silent. After a moment of quiet, he continued in a calmer tone. "As I say, I offered several select governments my secret. They thought it had potential but would not assist me. They were afraid that the United Nations would come to learn they were supporting it. The United Nations! A worthless organization!

So instead, they'll help me in other ways — innocent ways. If this scheme goes through, they will put the full resources of their states at my disposal. They guaranteed that. I can tell you this, these governments officially do not know of this plot and are quite willing to repudiate those people who are engaged in it. Indeed, if the truth be told, not one has not contributed a single ruble, mark, or forint to bring the plan to fruition. They have sent no word to me, but if they should agree, they said they would send a messenger. But for the first time, I am getting nervous. It isn't so much the fear of discovery that rattles me, but the sordid question of cash."

James shifted his weight, easing the tension in his muscles while maintaining contact with the wall. The man inside was more than just frustrated — he was desperate, cornered by his own ambition.

"The expenses are colossal and continuous," van Heerden complained. "But when I am successful, when it is working, all the money required will flow in. I'm sure of that. However, at present, I find myself with insufficient capital to go ahead much further. It is my intention to secure that capital in any way possible."

After a pause, van Heerden hung up the phone, followed by the sound of a chair scraping back and footsteps leaving the room. Putting down the Motel Kit, James extracted a slender tube from his jacket and sneaked to the window. He extended the small telescope with a silent twist of his wrist and peered through the glass into the living room. Along with the expected couch, chair, and small desk, it was dominated by two floor-to-ceiling bookcases, perhaps clues to a van Heerden's purpose.

His gaze swept over the spines of the books. One group seemed to comprise agricultural returns and reports from various countries around the globe. He focused on titles that appeared incongruous amidst the others: several tourist guidebooks from different nations of the world. Each book could be another piece of the puzzle, but James didn't know what the completed one even looked like. He retracted the telescope and replaced it in his pocket.

Interest in agriculture and geography could show many things, but combined with van Heerden's mysterious process, they hinted at something far-reaching, something worth the price of secrecy and subterfuge. What the endgame was, James couldn't even make a guess, but he could draw one conclusion. Van Heerden most certainly had murdered a man in the plain sight of a resort beach... it was clear that he was a player not to be underestimated.

The phone rang. James moved away from the window and replaced the transducer against the wall.

"Hello... yes, Hilda," van Heerden said. After a few seconds, he hissed out, "Trouble? What do you mean?" There was a long pause. "Is Bridgers still there? Good. Sending him away was smart. Is the other man still unconscious?" Another several moments of quiet before van Heerden spoke again. "No, I will take care of it. Are you positive he can't get loose? No, don't wait for me. Go back to the hotel. I don't want you identified when he regains consciousness." He hung up the phone.

Were they talking about Dakota? Have they captured him? The questions blazed through James' mind. He had to find out. Clearing in a single jump the wall dividing the two properties, he continued walking towards the front of the house, maintaining a relaxed, but quick, pace. When he reached his car, he turned away from van Heerden's house and pulled the paper from his back pocket. He studied it, glancing between it and the house multiple times before nodding in apparent satisfaction.

The door from the bungalow behind him closed with a soft thud as James climbed into the driver's seat. He kept his eyes on the rearview mirror, watching van Heerden move with urgency to his car. The sedan revved up, its headlights pierced through the gathering twilight. After waiting for him to drive a few blocks ahead, James made a U-turn to follow.

James was now grateful that Smith had rented this unremarkable, bland sedan for him. In the dim light of the early evening, it almost disappeared into the surrounding traffic. James reviewed training scenarios in his mind, attempting to plan on how to rescue Dakota, if he indeed was the captive van Heerden mentioned.

The trip was brief, concluding at a plain warehouse sandwiched between two other structures, with alleys on either side. James drove past while van Heerden parked in front before turning the corner and spotting Dakota's motorcycle next to the curb. He pulled behind it.

With a quick and fluid movement, James slipped out of his car and made his way towards the warehouse. He moved to the back of the building by the alley next to it, careful not to make a sound. He scanned the wall of windows. One was ajar. Slipping down the wall, he peered through the grimy glass. Only a single lamp was on the inside, high in the ceiling.

In that sterile circle of light, Dakota lay bound on a refrigerator dolly, his hands tied behind his back. Two thick straps held his body in place, one wrapped tightly around his chest and the other securing his ankles. A handkerchief was shoved unceremoniously into his mouth. Dakota's leather jacket lay on the dirty floor next to him. His eyes were fixed on van Heerden holding a gun on him.

"I will remove the gag. Any attempt to make a loud sound will be your last," van Heerden's voice was cold. "You are to answer my questions. Is that understood?"

Dakota gave a nod of agreement. Van Heerden leaned down and yanked the gag from Dakota's mouth, causing him to spit out a few stray fibers.

"First the obvious question," van Heerden said. "What are you doing in here?"

"I was looking to score," Dakota responded.

"To steal something? There is nothing in here to take," van Heerden waved around the empty room, "which you could obviously see through the windows. Why did you come in? Why were you discovered peering into the office?"

"That lab?" Dakota answered. "Okay, man, I'll lay it on you straight. I was aiming to cop some free junk."

"You use heroin?" van Heerden's eyebrow arched as he scrutinized Dakota's stoic face, searching for cracks in the facade. The question hung between them, laced with his skepticism.

"Yeah, man," Dakota admitted.

With a grunt of suspicion, van Heerden squatted next to Dakota and yanked his arm toward him, examining the inside of his elbow to reveal unmarred skin. His fingers prodded for evidence, finding none. He did the same with Dakota's other arm. "You bear no needle marks on your arms. Also, you would have already sold that nice leather jacket to pay for a hit. Not to mention you are in far too good physical shape to be a heroin addict. I would believe steroids, however."

He stood and circled Dakota like a hunter sizing up prey caught in a trap. His tone was sarcastic, a mocking smile playing on his lips as he leaned down. "Do you want to try again? Nothing more? Not even a plea for mercy before we continue with some more persuasive questioning?"

Dakota met van Heerden's gaze evenly, the set of his jaw betraying no fear. He shook his head.

James' hand squeezed the frame of the window with an iron grip. Time slowed to a crawl as he struggled with the impulse to burst through the glass and rescue Dakota. But he knew it would be a foolish move. He wasn't armed. Without a weapon, they would both be dead in seconds. He had to think of something else.

"Very well. You force me to go to the next part of our game." Van Heerden stuffed the gag back into Dakota's mouth. "We don't want anybody calling the police because of your screams disturbing the peace."

Van Heerden looked the room over. He made his way towards a circuit box on the wall and picked up two cables coming from it, bare cords protruding from the ends. With deliberate cruelty, he approached Dakota and wrapped the exposed wires around the metal frame of the dolly in a meticulous fashion. When he finished, he returned to the circuit box. "Nod your head if you change your mind and wish to cooperate."

James narrowed his eyes from his concealed vantage point. He knew the stakes had just been raised: van Heerden was going to use electrical shock to force Dakota to talk. James had a limited amount of time to act.

His gaze darted across the exterior wall of the warehouse until finally settling on a gray steel box: the breaker panel for the building. James didn't waste any time and immediately ran towards it. He pulled open the cabinet door as quietly as he could and placed his hand on the switch, his heart pounding with nerves. Cutting the power now could alert van Heerden that somebody else was around. His plan was to wait, to fool van Heerden into thinking his do-it-yourself torture device blew a fuse.

He made a silent apology to Dakota. He listened, keeping the window he left in sight, calculating how much time he had to get inside.

Then, a muffled scream pierced the silence — a guttural sound of raw pain that punched James right in the gut. Without hesitation, he yanked down the lever on the breaker panel, cutting the power to the building. For good measure, he flipped a few of the breakers as well. "Please," he prayed under his breath, "let this work."

Racing back to the window, James checked through the glass. In the blackness, van Heerden's cursing echoed off the walls in a storm of confusion and fury. A flurry of clicking the switch on and off at the circuit box followed. His footsteps thudded towards the door, seeking the cause of the sudden outage. Van Heerden disappeared toward the rear of the warehouse, his outline swallowed by the darkness. This was it — James' only chance. He slipped inside the warehouse.

"Stay quiet," he whispered to Dakota, lips barely moving as he worked swiftly to release the straps that held his partner to the refrigerator dolly.

It took a second for Dakota to focus on James, then he nodded. His face was wet with perspiration and his breathing was heavy. Despite that, his expression was steel-hard despite the ordeal.

With a final tug, the restraints fell away. James pulled Dakota to his feet. He staggered for a moment, then steadied himself. James draped Dakota's jacket over his shoulders, concealing his bound hands. The two hurried to the street door.

Stepping outside the warehouse, James pulled out the gag. He threw it down the sidewalk, opposite where they were going. "Maybe he'll think you escaped that way." He pointed. "My car is parked in back of your bike. Go. I'll be behind you."

Dakota sprinted along the concrete pathway. With a quick flick of his wrist, James drew out his pocketknife and punctured the front sidewall of van Heerden's sedan. The air let out a loud hiss as the tire deflated. Smirking, James took off down the street.

He rounded the corner and went over to Dakota. Reaching under the coat, he cut the ropes. Dakota turned to James, rubbing his wrists.

"Thanks, man," Dakota grinned.

James returned the grin. "Service with a smile, that's my motto. Are you okay? Are you able to ride? "

Dakota nodded as he slipped on his jacket. "Yeah. Though I was seeing sparks there for a moment."

"Follow me." James put away his pocketknife and headed for the driver's door of his car. "We'll find someplace to debrief."

After a short time, James pulled into the Majorette Drive-In, Dakota close behind on his sleek motorcycle. The place was bustling with teenagers. Their laughter and chatter competed with the Beatles' song *Help* blaring from the jukebox. The neon lights of the sign reflected off the shiny paint jobs of cars and hot rods parked around the lot.

The young secret agents joined in as though just another pair of teens out for the night, though James' tailored sports jacket and slacks stood out among the casual jeans and t-shirts of the other guys. As they approached the window, Dakota caught the attention of a group of boys who eagerly asked questions about his impressive bike.

James placed their order for burgers and fries before leading them to an isolated table away from the crowds. The rich, greasy aroma of sizzling meat wafted through the air as the two sat down. James switched to Cherokee. "What happened?"

"Miss Glaum — "

"Hilda." James took a drink of his soda. "Her first name is Hilda. She called van Heerden while I was listening in. I followed him to you."

"I'm glad you did. Well, Hilda baby delivered some bottles of chemicals to the warehouse. The office there is set up as some kind of laboratory... or factory, I don't know which." Dakota took a bite of his burger and propped his elbows on the table. "There's a chemist that works there... a man named Bridgers, a real coke-head."

"No idea what's being cooked up?" James popped a french fry into his mouth. "Drugs?"

Dakota shook his head. "I don't know. I was trying to get a look inside when someone hit me from behind... POW! Lights out."

"Somebody sneaked up on you?" James grinned. "Why, that's hard to believe. I didn't think that was possible, Mister Kitty Ears."

"I'll let that pass since you saved me from glowing like a light bulb," Dakota said. "Anyway, that's all I have. What about you? Any idea what he's up to?"

James wadded up the greasy burger wrapper and dropped it in the plastic basket. He leaned forward with an intensity that sharpened the blue of his eyes to a glacial hue. "No. More questions than answers. Van Heerden's bookcase is stuffed with books on agriculture and travel guides."

"It could be he's a frustrated farmer."

"Doubtful." James used a napkin to rub the french fry salt off his fingers. "And what does a laboratory and chemicals have to do with it? It could be his reading material and the lab may be unrelated." He shook his head. "One thing is certain, though. Van Heerden's in a corner with his finances. When he was on the phone, he complained he was running out of cash. He's angling for some assistance from a foreign government."

"Which one?"

"He didn't say." James finished his soda.

"Money troubles? We could use that." Dakota's brown eyes reflected his understanding, the analytical gears turning in his head.

"Exactly." James' mind raced through various plans like a chess grandmaster several moves ahead. "We can use that. He's frantic enough to take risks. That's our opening."

Dakota shrugged. "You're on your own. My cover's toast, man."

"Unfortunate choice of terms after what you just went through." James cocked an eyebrow.

"Hilarious. At any rate, I gotta lie low for a while. They could easily identify me." Dakota wiped his mouth with a napkin, not one of his movements wasted. "What's the play?"

James thought for a moment. "Have Smith create a bank account for me — fifty grand should do it."

Dakota almost choked on a fry. "Fifty grand! From Smith? You've got to be crazy! He'll howl."

"Let him." James flashed a sweet smile. "I'm counting on your considerable charm to talk him into it." He dipped a fry into a small cup of ketchup. "Besides, he likes you better."

"Huh. He's probably still mad at you because you bugged his office and he couldn't find it."

James shrugged. "Hey, the training assignment was to plant a listening device. It didn't exclude any location. Specifically."

Dakota grinned. "The account under whose name?"

"Mine. I'm going to get close to Hilda and pose as an investor for van Heerden's scheme. I'll be as desperate for money as he is. She may help to unravel this. I'll dream up a new identity, something credible yet disposable. The Swedish business student bit won't fly with her." He paused. "How about this? I'll be a rich orphan —" James stumbled over the word, although it was better than the truth: abandoned. " — running out of funds."

"That could work." Dakota's voice was firm, the certainty in his tone echoing their reliance on each other's capabilities formed during training. "You know, I don't know which one is more dangerous... me asking

Smith for 50 grand or you contacting Hilda. I'll get in touch with Smith tonight, even if it means waking him up from his beauty sleep. Also, I'll run background checks on Hilda Glaum and Bridgers."

"And something else…"

Dakota arched his eyebrows in a question.

"Nose around the commodities market. See if you can pick up any rumors," James said.

"Commodities? Like corn, wheat, soybeans? Stuff like that?" Dakota asked. "What does that have to do with anything?"

"I have no idea. Stardt's desk at the hotel had commodity price charts and papers holding calculations," James said. "It may be off the wall, but I'm wondering if there is any possible connection to van Heerden's taste in library books."

Dakota nodded. "I'll add that to my list."

"Excellent." James' eyes were already scanning the drive-in, and the street outside, always vigilant. "Let me know when the account is ready."

"Agreed. Expect a message from your travel agent when everything is arranged." Dakota switched back to English. "Let's remember this place. They make really fine burgers here."

Chapter Five

JAMES WAITED FOR THE head bellman to finish with other guests at his desk before he strolled up.

"Morning, Marty," James said. Marty looked up, attentive and eager to assist.

"Can I help you with anything, ah, particular, Mr. Vagus?" Marty grinned, the insider on the joke.

James played along. "Do you have any... information about whom we spoke about the other day?"

"Miss Glaum?" Marty lowered his voice. "The party in question is due to check out at the end of the week."

"That doesn't give me much time."

"I know it doesn't, sir." Marty gave a wink.

James didn't realize he had spoken out loud. He needed to be aware of that in the future. He dropped into a confidential tone. "Does the... party in question have any routines? Ones I may find myself... involved in? I don't know, maybe become part of? By coincidence, you understand. Just accidental. Have you noticed any?"

"Well, she usually goes to the pool in the late morning." Marty checked at his watch. "Should be there in about an hour or so."

"Good. When she heads out today, would it be possible for you to give me a call in my room? So I don't miss her." James winked back.

"Why, of course, Mr. Vagus." Marty flashed a knowing grin. "I'll let you know as soon as she's on her way."

"Thanks, Marty." James turned to leave, stopped, then leaned toward Marty. He kept his voice hopeful, but nonchalant. "Oh, is there any chance you could make sure the lounge chair next to hers stays vacant for me?"

Marty considered the request for a moment before nodding. "I believe Carlos, the pool attendant, could arrange that, but he might need some... consideration."

"Of course. This should be enough... for both of you," James said, reaching into his wallet and sliding two twenty-dollar bills into Marty's waiting hand.

"Thank you, Mr. Vagus. I'll see to it myself." Marty pocketed the money and walked away.

James went to the newsstand, bought *The Wall Street Journal*, and returned to his hotel room. After changing into his swimsuit, he took a nondescript black attaché case out of the closet and set it on the bed. Unlocking it, he opened it to reveal a compact radio station. Now to wait.

The phone call pulled James out of his restless pacing in the room. He snatched it up, heart racing. "This is Vagus."

"She passed by on the way to the pool," Marty said, his tone conspiratorial. "And your lounge chair is all ready, Mr. Vagus."

"Perfect. Thank you." James hung up and went to the radio. Setting the frequency dial, he picked up the mike and pushed the transmit button. "Foxhound to Shadowhawk... Foxhound to Shadowhawk come in, please."

"This is Shadowhawk, Go ahead, Foxhound," Dakota's calm voice crackled through the speaker.

"Shadowhawk, it's go time. Get ready." Excitement tinged James' tone.

"Copy that," Dakota said. "The account is active now, although Smith screamed like I was taking out his appendix without anesthetic. First Florida Bank, under your name. We're good to go."

"Copy. Give me about twenty minutes," James said. "Foxhound out."

"Copy. Shadowhawk out."

After locking the attaché case and stowing it in the closet, James draped a towel around his neck.

He grabbed his sunglasses, newspaper, and made his way toward the pool. As he walked through the lobby, Marty was busy with another guest, but still gave a grin and a thumbs up in James' direction. James reciprocated with a smile of his own.

He slipped his shades on before stepping onto the pool deck. Scanning the area, James caught sight of Hilda, stretched out on a lounge chair and basking in the warm Miami sun. Her golden hair spilled over her shoulders, and her lithe body was clad in a red bikini that left little to the imagination. She looked every bit the femme fatale, and James couldn't help but admire the way she commanded attention without even trying. His tip to Carlos had paid off: a lounge chair next to her was unoccupied.

"Stay sharp," he told himself, taking a deep breath. He called up the image of suave movie star Cary Grant the other night to help him on his date. He did it one more time. "You've got this. Come on, Cary, time for a repeat performance."

James strolled toward Hilda with slow, assured strides, almost a swagger. His nerves tingled as he neared the vacant lounger.

"Is this free?" he asked with a casual smile, gesturing to the empty seat.

"Be my guest," Hilda purred, pushing her sunglasses up to reveal shrewd, calculating green eyes.

"Thank you." James settled into the lounger, tossing the newspaper on the concrete. He stretched out his muscular legs and folded his hands over his stomach. He took a moment to soak in the sun, the scent of chlorine and sunscreen mixed in with the salt air. Then he turned to Hilda as he picked up the paper. "Beautiful morning, isn't it?"

"It is." She glanced at *The Wall Street Journal*, then appraised him as if he was a horse she was going to bet on in the next race. "So you are here on school vacation, Mr....?" she trailed off, arching an eyebrow in an unasked question.

"Vagus. James Vagus." He extended a hand, and she shook it, her grip firm and confident.

"Call me Hilda." She smiled.

"Alright, Hilda. And no, I don't attend college."

She nodded at the newspaper. "You don't read that for pleasure, I'm sure. For work, then?"

James pretended to shudder. "Please! The terms 'work' and 'job' are not in my vocabulary."

She chuckled. "Then tell me, James, what brings a charming young man like you to Miami?"

He leaned toward her, as though sharing a secret. "Adventure," he confided in a low voice. Sometimes the truth was the best lie.

"Isn't that what we're all searching for? That... and romance," Hilda's eyes locked on his as if she were trying to probe his mind. "Well, I hope you find what you're looking for, James Vagus."

"Believe me," he said. He returned her piercing gaze with a confident grin. "I think I just might have."

Hilda picked up a Bloody Mary from the small table next to her lounger. She took a sip. "Would you care for a cocktail?"

James returned a smile. "No, thank you. I don't drink."

"Not of legal age?" she teased.

"True, I have a few years to go yet, but that's only a part of the reason," James said.

Hilda's eyes darted to the silver cross hanging around James' neck. She offered him another smile, both coy and inviting, leaving James to wonder just how much of this dance she had orchestrated herself.

The opening moves in the chess match had been executed. The pieces were placed on the board, and the two players settled back on their loungers. The sun bore down, casting glimmering patterns across the pool's shimmering surface, shattered when a guest dove in. Hilda sipped her cocktail with an air of calculated casualness. James' heart raced beneath his seemingly calm exterior, very aware of how high the stakes were in this delicate game. One false move and his first mission will be a failure.

"Commodities, commodities," he said to himself as he picked up *The Wall Street Journal* and paged through it. Out of the corner of his eye, he spotted Hilda's glass stop momentarily on its way to her lips.

"Mr. Vagus? Mr. James Vagus?" A pool attendant, wearing a "Carlos" name tag, strolled along the line of loungers, holding an extension telephone in his hand. "Mr. Vagus?"

James raised his hand. "Here."

Carlos came up to the lounger. "You have a call, sir."

"Ah, thank you." James forced a casual smile, accepting the phone and waiting until Carlos plugged it into a nearby jack. He lifted the handset. "This is Vagus."

"This is Mr. Smith, Mr. Vagus. Do you remember who I am?" Dakota's voice blasted through the earpiece.

James grimaced and held the receiver away from his ear, positioning it so Hilda couldn't help but overhear the conversation. He rolled his eyes. "Of course I do, Mr. Smith," he said in a bored, weary voice. "You are the executor of my trust fund. Are you going to berate me for my profligate spending habits again?"

"Yes, Mr. Vagus, I am," Dakota snapped. "I've been going over the numbers, and I must say I'm very alarmed. Your trust is running toward the red. At the rate you're burning through it, you will have not a dime left when you turn 21. You'll end up standing on the street corner, holding a tin cup!"

"Really? Well, that will never do." James reacted in a sarcastic show of surprise and concern.

"Indeed. You'll need to replenish it soon, or — heaven forbid — you may actually have to work for a living." Dakota's tone held a note of mock disapproval that was almost too convincing.

"As would you, too." James' retort provoked a wordless, angry sputtering from Dakota.

"Don't be flippant with me, Mr. Vagus!" Dakota's voice came out of the receiver like a flamethrower.

"Don't worry, Mr. Smith, I'll figure something out," James went on in a more assuring tone, his eyes flicking toward Hilda. She appeared to be listening while pretending not to. He waved the *Journal* as if Dakota could see it over the phone. "I'm on the track of some investments which should provide a decent return —
"

"See that you do. Or else I'm putting you on an allowance even a fifth grader would find cheap!" Dakota shouted, before hanging up.

"Have a nice day," James smirked as he replaced the receiver, taking a moment to gather his thoughts. He turned to Hilda. "Sorry. Mr. Smith sometimes speaks in a rather, um, vigorous way."

"He's your business manager?"

"Trust administrator," James corrected. "My parents were killed in a car crash, and they left me an inheritance. Many describe it as 'sizeable'. It seems I've been enjoying life a little too much of late. Not applying myself to those... well, other words. The ones not in my vocabulary."

"Is that so?" Hilda lowered her sunglasses to look at him, calculating.

James grinned a response. He continued, his voice tinged with just the right amount of frustration. "It seems I need to replenish the funds, but the thought of doing actual work?" He shrugged. "Well, that's not very appealing."

"Perhaps I can help," Hilda was quiet for a moment, as though considering the possibilities — and James' qualifications. "I have some connections that might assist you with your... financial predicament."

"Really?" James feigned delight as if the idea had never occurred to him. "I'd be eternally grateful if you could introduce me to these... connections of yours."

"Consider it done," Hilda flashed a mysterious smile, her eyes glinting with an unreadable emotion. "You must be prepared for anything, James Vagus. The path to fortune isn't always what it appears."

"I pride myself on being very flexible," he said, his heart pounding with adrenaline and excitement.

"Tell me," Hilda said, stirring her Bloody Mary with the celery stalk before taking a sip. "How much money do you have left to invest?"

"About $50,000," James said in a casual tone, paying close attention to her reaction. She didn't flinch at the figure, which he took as a promising sign.

"Perfect," she said, her voice sultry yet with the calculating clinks of a calculator. "Can you get it in cash?"

"Cash?"

"Yes. It reduces the... paperwork, shall we say." She put the celery in her mouth and crunched down.

James thought for a moment. "I suppose I could. But I'd need a couple of days to arrange it."

"Excellent. Then I think I can get you in touch with someone who can help you turn your investment into something more substantial," Hilda said.

"Who would that be?" James leaned closer.

Hilda glanced around to ensure no one was eavesdropping. She lowered her voice. "His name is van Heerden. A man of many talents and connections."

"Interesting," James tried to sound intrigued rather than eager. "What kind of business is he involved in?"

"Let's just say he knows how to make money flow like a river," came Hilda's cryptic response. "If you're serious about this, I can arrange a meeting."

"Consider me serious," James responded with a confident smile.

"Alright then," Hilda said, rising from her lounge chair with grace. "I'll contact van Heerden and set something up. Just remember, James, in this game, there are no guarantees. Are you willing to take that risk?"

James looked into her eyes, the intensity of his gaze unwavering. "I wouldn't have it any other way. Risk is my middle name."

"Good," Hilda's eyes gleamed with approval. "I'll be in touch."

"I'm in room 110," James said.

For a brief second, Hilda reacted to the number — the room next to the one that belonged to Stardt. She recovered and sauntered away. James couldn't help but feel a surge of satisfaction.

***

Two days later, James stepped out of his car in front of a restaurant, taking in the elegant white building before him. Its two-story structure boasted a Spanish influence, evident in the terracotta clay tiles lining the roof to the urns that adorned each corner. A lone red neon sign protruded from the second floor, declaring "Cafe", making the suggestion it was nothing more than a cheap roadside diner.

As James scanned the lot, he spotted Dakota's motorcycle parked among the cars. But as always, Dakota himself was nowhere to be seen, becoming a shadow of the night. James stood tall and squared his shoulders. It was getting easier pretending to be someone else.

When he entered the seafood restaurant, the rich and inviting aroma of garlic and butter enveloped him, mingled with the hum of conversation reverberating off the ceilings. The dining room stretched two stories high and was adorned with wrought iron, Spanish-style chandeliers that cast a warm glow throughout. Pristine white tablecloths draped each table, and waiters glided between them like graceful specters, anticipating every need of their guests. And there, at the entrance, stood Hilda in all her splendor, dressed in a sleek black dress that accentuated her beauty. Upon spotting James, she greeted him with a radiant smile and beckoned him over to her side.

"Ah, Mr. Vagus." She offered her hand. "So punctual."

"Always." James pressed a brief kiss to her knuckles before allowing her to lead him to their table.

"Were you able to obtain the funds?"

James tapped the breast pocket of his suit jacket. "I have them right here."

"Excellent. Mr. van Heerden is waiting," Hilda nodded toward a shadowy corner booth. A man sat there, nursing a glass of red wine, his features obscured by the dim lighting. As they approached, his face came into view — the same one James had seen on the beach with Stardt.

"Mr. Van Heerden, I presume?" James asked, extending his hand.

"Indeed." The man shook it, his grip firm and assured. He gestured for James to take a seat. "And you must be James Vagus. Hilda has told me about your... investment needs."

"Ah, yes," James said as he sat. "I understand you're the man to see about making money without breaking a sweat."

"Something like that." Van Heerden's eyes narrowed as he studied James. He chuckled. "But I am compelled to ask, are you prepared to take risks for high rewards? We only deal in cash, and our business is not for the faint of heart."

"Risks don't scare me," James said with confidence, meeting van Heerden's gaze head-on. "Now, let's talk details. What exactly am I investing in?"

Van Heerden leaned back in his seat, swirling the wine in his glass as he considered his response. "Well, Mr. Vagus, now that would be telling," he said with a sly smile. "You can be assured, your investment will be well-protected and profitable."

James matched van Heerden's smile. "I need a little more information. Is it to recover golden ingots from the sunken ships of the Spanish Armada? For companies setting forth to harness the horsepower of the sea to run factories? Or for optimistic enterprises that discovered uranium deposits in the deserts of New Mexico?" He carefully watched for the reaction to the next suggestion. "I don't really care what it is, if it brings in money. Even something as dull as, say, parking lots or farming."

The right corner of van Heerden's lip twitched ever so slightly. "Let us say you are investing in a new chemical process. It promises to pay millions when it is used."

"I know nothing about chemistry. I don't mind admitting that to you," James said. "I am also a child in matters of finance. Maybe I shouldn't bother about the details as long as you send my dividends on time." After a moment of deliberation, he pulled an envelope from his jacket pocket and placed it on the table. "Here's the $50,000. In cash, as requested."

"Excellent." Van Heerden reached for the money.

James maintained pressure on the envelope with his hand. "I need a receipt."

Van Heerden's flinty gaze locked onto James' eyes. "A receipt?"

"Fifty thousand is a lot of dollars. The administrator of my trust account would insist. He can be quite difficult." James spoke to Hilda without breaking eye contact with van Heerden. "Can't he, Hilda?"

"Yes," Hilda answered in a flat, disinterested voice.

"I wonder how much of a child you are in reality, Mr. Vagus," van Heerden said after a pause. "You're wise beyond your youth."

"It must have been my upbringing," James replied in a cool tone. He slipped his free hand into his suit coat and extracted a folded sheet of paper. He laid it on the table.

Van Heerden flashed a tight smile. After glancing at the sentences written on the page, he pulled out a gold fountain pen from his jacket pocket. He signed the receipt with a flair.

"Thank you, Mr. van Heerden." James picked up the receipt while releasing his grip on the envelope. "Oh, and my bank account information is with the money. So you know where to deposit the dividends."

"Of course." His eyes gleaming, van Heerden took the money and slipped it into his own jacket. "Welcome to the Golden Syndicate, Mr. Vagus. You won't regret it."

"No, I don't think I will," James said. They sealed the deal with a handshake.

"Now, I recommend the lobster," van Heerden said with a smile.

The dinner conversation between the three was on any topic other than van Heerden's "Golden Syndicate". James decided not to press for more information at the moment, so he went on playing the role of the spoiled rich orphan. And van Heerden was correct. The lobster was delicious.

Chapter Six

THE SUN BLAZED OVER the Miami Beach Marina as James approached the Usurper, a sleek, 25-foot saltwater fishing boat that stood out among the others with its glossy white hull and polished silver railings. He stopped by the stern.

"Uh… hello? Anybody onboard? Ah… ahoy?" James called out.

Dakota came out of the cabin dressed as the skipper. He wore deck shoes without socks, jeans, and an unbuttoned tropic print shirt billowing in the breeze. His long hair was hidden under a baseball cap adorned with an embroidered marlin. An unlit cigar butt was clenched in his teeth.

"Good morning, Captain," James said, stepping onto the boat. "Um… permission to come aboard?"

Dakota granted it with a wave of his hand. "You James Vagus?"

"Yes."

Dakota eyed the way James was dressed: smart sports coat, slacks, and an open-collar shirt. "Did you come for some deep-sea fishing or to attend a board of directors meeting?"

"Why... fishing," James said, playing along with the charade of having chartered the vessel himself.

"I hope you don't mind splattering fish guts over your nice pretty clothes," Dakota took the cigar out of his mouth and pitched it overboard. "The other party canceled, so it's just you. Lay to and cast off the stern line."

James stood there, confused.

"Take the rope at the back of the boat off the post on the dock," Dakota explained to James, pronouncing every word.

"Oh."

As James took care of the rope at the stern, Dakota cast off the bow line. Taking the wheel, Dakota pulled out of the marina and headed out into the open ocean. James joined his partner in the cockpit.

"Nice vessel," James said as he studied the boat's layout as they picked up speed.

"Yeah. I thought I'd upgrade our meeting spots," Dakota said.

"I wouldn't mind owning one of these someday."

"Start saving your pennies now, James." Dakota's eyes scanned the horizon as they gained distance from the shore. "This baby doesn't come cheap."

"Is that so?" James asked. "Did you rent it?"

"Truth is, this craft belongs to the CIA. They use it for surveillance off Cuba, as well as some injection of personnel there," Dakota said.

"They must be better funded than MIS-X," James dryly said, glancing around the elegant vessel.

Their journey continued farther out into the ocean until the once prominent land was reduced to a thin line on the distant horizon. The powerful engine of the Usurper roared as Dakota controlled its speed, matching the rhythmic waves that rocked against the hull. He throttled back. They returned to the deck and sat on two bolted-down chairs.

"Alright, time to fill you in on last night's dinner meeting." James recounted the events, describing what he had learned about van Heerden's scheme — the Golden Syndicate. "It involves some sort of chemical process. I got little more than that, but it's not something we can ignore."

"Chemical process, huh?" Dakota mused, fingers drumming against the chair arm as he considered the implications. "That adds up. I did some digging on our friend Bridgers. Turns out he's a brilliant chemist, but his drug addiction has caused him to lose one job after another."

"Sounds like that makes him the perfect pawn for van Heerden," James observed, his mind turning over the possibilities. "But what does all this have to do with the Golden Syndicate? More to the point, *what* is it? We only have a name."

Dakota shrugged. "It seems a few pieces of the puzzle have been kicked under the sofa. But one thing's certain — we need to find out more about this chemical process and what it could mean for... well, whoever's on the wrong end of it."

James nodded.

"I've also dug up some dirt on Hilda," Dakota went on. "Turns out she isn't your average socialite."

"Really? I'm shocked. Shocked!" James said sarcastically. "Although I never thought she was. What's the scoop?"

Dakota leaned toward James before continuing. "She lives in a fancy... and very expensive... Manhattan apartment, but has no visible means of financial support. Records show that she's been involved in confidence games and blackmail schemes in the past."

"Convicted of anything?"

"No." Dakota sat back. "She's out of the action far enough to keep her away from prison."

"So she's most likely a freelance grifter who hires out for the highest bidder," James said. "That would explain why I thought her relationship with van Heerden was like to an employee and employer. That's what she is."

"But there's something else you should know. Smith passed on a tip about a likely lead in Vienna. An informant approached the embassy there with information that mentioned van Heerden's name. The contact refused to elaborate further, but left instructions on how to set up another meeting."

"Vienna?" James echoed. "That could mean the van Heerden's operation is international. You think it's worth following up on?"

"Smith does," Dakota replied. "I'll fly out as soon as we're done here. With any luck, this informant can fill in some gaps in our knowledge."

"You get to go to Vienna?" James complained. "See? I always knew Smith liked you best."

Dakota laughed. "I'll bring you back a souvenir. Perhaps a plump sausage."

"You know what you can do with — "

Suddenly, the roar of an engine caught their attention. A speedboat skimmed across the swells, charging straight towards them at full throttle.

"Keep your guard up," Dakota murmured. "This is suspicious."

"Agreed." James shaded his eyes with one hand as he tried to make out the approaching boat. "I'm getting that same feeling — wait!" He spotted the glint of sunlight reflecting off a gun barrel being raised. "Down!"

An ear-shattering roar ripped through the air as a barrage of machine gun fire shattered the silence. James and Dakota flung themselves to the deck, scrambling for cover behind the gunwale as deadly bullets sliced through the air with ferocious speed. James' heart was pounding so hard he could feel it thumping against his chest. He couldn't believe they were still alive amidst this onslaught of flying lead.

A violent explosion of metal and glass obliterated the Usurper's controls, sending shrapnel flying in all directions. For some reason, James thought the noise of shooting sounded louder now than when he was practicing on the firing range. Maybe it depends on which end of the barrel you're on, he figured. He battled through the fear coursing through his system.

"This is a CIA boat!" James shouted. "Doesn't this thing have a bazooka or something?"

"No! I told you, this is for surveillance only!" Dakota yelled back.

The speedboat rode the choppy waves like a wild beast, circling its target with deadly precision. Another swarm of bullets ripped through the air, pulverizing the boat's controls and radio.

"Why aren't they aiming for us through the hull?" James said. "It's fiberglass. A machine gun could tear through it like it was paper."

The answer came when a grenade dropped onto the deck with a dull thud. James acted on instinct, diving for the explosive before it could go off. He grabbed hold of the metal pineapple and rolled away to safety. With all his strength, he flung the grenade over the side of the ship, causing it to detonate in a powerful blast that sent a massive wave shooting into the air and soaking him in cold water.

"They don't want our bullet-ridden corpses to wash up on shore," James said. "May cause questions. I think they want us to go down with the ship."

"Well, we'll accommodate them. Let's dive in." Dakota army crawled toward the cabin.

The speedboat circled the boat once more. A thump echoed from the bow, followed by an explosion that rocked the entire vessel. The Usurper shook violently as if lifted into the air by an invisible hand, before crashing back down on the waves.

"Dakota?" James called.

"Okay!" came the reply.

The speedboat's motor came to a halt. James peeked over the side with caution. The two men sat in the other boat some distance off, observing the Usurper. To James' utter amazement, one of them pulled out two beers and passed a can to his companion. Both popped open their brews and settled in to watch the sinking. A scrape of metal against the deck drew James' attention away from the sight. Dakota was returning from the cabin, wet.

"That last one got us," Dakota said. "Punched a hole in the hull. We're going down by the bow."

Dakota had already shed his cap, shirt, and shoes. He pushed a pair of weight belts and two Lambertson Diving Units in front of him. The devices were equipped with air tanks for underwater use, as well as an extra chest tank that filtered out carbon dioxide. This let a diver breathe while not creating any bubbles that would give away his location at the surface. Dakota also had the cord of a small bundle looped around one foot.

Remaining on his side below the gunwale, James took off his jacket. "They're still out there, waiting for us to imitate the Titanic." He ripped his shirt off, the popped buttons tapping and skipping across the deck. "They want to make sure we drown." He worked on getting his shoes and socks off.

James and Dakota struggled with the diving equipment, trying to fasten the gear while lying in awkward positions on their sides. Water rushed in from the front of the boat, swiftly flooding the cabin. The deck to begin to list.

"It looks like those guys' view will be blocked as the stern rises," Dakota said. "Wait until then to bail."

James nodded. The two put on the gas mask-like face coverings and turned the valve of the air tanks. And they waited.

The boat tilted at a steep angle, causing unsecured objects to crash and slide around the deck. James grabbed onto the pedestal of one chair bolted to the deck for stability while also gripping Dakota's hand, wincing in pain as if his arms were being yanked out of their sockets. The bow dipped underwater and waves started splashing over the port side.

Dakota's voice came muffled through the mask. "Now!"

James let go of Dakota's hand. His partner slid and tumbled down the slanted deck before rolling over the side of the boat and diving under the water. James followed suit, and they both swam away from the Usurper, disappearing into the depths below. After a few minutes, the ocean swallowed the wreckage of the boat, leaving only a flurry of bubbles and debris to mark its last location.

The weight belts they wore on their waists kept them submerged. James treaded water, anxious, waiting on the next move of the men in the boat. Would they believe he and Dakota drowned?

The sound of the speedboat's engines rumbled above, churning the ocean. The speedboat roared to where the Usurper went down, then crisscrossed the area a few times before leaving. At last, the droning hum of the engines faded into the distance.

Dakota tapped James on the arm and pointed to his foot. The bundle's cord still was wrapped around his ankle. James removed it, and Dakota indicated up. James released the buckle on his weight belt, allowing it to sink into the depths below. Dakota mirrored his actions, and together they began their ascent toward the sun.

When they broke through the waves, Dakota tugged a ripcord on the bundle. A burst of compressed air sounded, and a float inflated, looking like a rubber surfboard.

"Man, that was too close," Dakota's voice was tinged with exhaustion as he took off the Lambertson Diving Unit. He let it slip beneath the surface and clung to the inflatable.

James nodded in agreement, his eyes scanning the horizon for any sign of danger. He removed the diving gear and also released it to sink to the bottom of the Atlantic. He joined Dakota, hanging onto the float. "Alright, time to paddle our way back to shore."

"Sure beats waiting around for a rescue that's never gonna come," Dakota said. "I don't think those two called the Coast Guard."

James allowed himself a small smile. "Now we know how van Heerden spent part of that 50000 dollars I gave him. He hired those goons. It looks like he has a pattern for handling investors. Grab their cash, then bump them off. Saves having to pay those pesky dividends."

"Let's get moving," Dakota said. "We've got a long way to go."

Kicking their feet, they began their arduous journey back to the safety of dry land.

"This reminds me of that obstacle course we ran in training," James said after a few minutes. "Remember? I carried you across the finish line."

Dakota shook his head. "I think you're misremembering, James. I pulled *you* across the finish line."

James chuckled. "Okay, let's say we dragged each other across the finish line."

"That's more accurate." Dakota grinned.

The two paddled in the shore's direction in silence for a little longer.

"Dakota," James asked, "were you scared? When they were shooting at us?"

Dakota met James' gaze. "Absolutely terrified."

"Yeah, I was, too. Even so, I trusted in you... in us... that we would get through it," James said.

"Me, too."

The pair's journey toward land went on in quiet. After several minutes, James spoke again, trying to lighten his mood. "You know, if a shark would eat you right about now, I'd be the one who gets to travel to Vienna."

"Actually, James," Dakota said, as though giving the matter deep thought, "you resemble a plump seal more than I do."

"That's muscle, not fat."

"Shark wouldn't know."

As they continued paddling, each one took turns explaining in great detail why the other would be a more tasty shark snack. At last, James and Dakota staggered out of the surf to the damp sands of the shore. Their muscles ached, and their lungs burned from exertion, but they had made it.

Several of the beachgoers were staring at them as they emerged from the waves. James realized how odd they must look. Neither wore a shirt nor shoes, but were dressed in regular pants and dragging a rubber surfboard behind them.

A nearby boy stared at them as if they were strange humanoid amphibians emerging from the deep. Dakota held out the float. "Do you want this? We don't need it anymore."

"Yeah! Thanks, mister!" The kid ran up, grabbed the inflatable, and rushed into the waves.

James clucked his tongue. "Naughty boy. Giving away government equipment like that."

"He'll be a taxpayer one day," Dakota said.

"I'm going to return to the hotel," James said, his voice hoarse but steady. "I'll try to have a little chat with Hilda."

"Okay. I'll telephone any updates from Vienna to Aunt Martha," Dakota said.

"Understood." James took a step toward the Ocean View, then halted. He turned back to Dakota. "Oh, nimm keinen Holzstrudel."

Dakota hesitated. "My German isn't as good as yours, but did you just say..."

James grinned. "Don't take any wooden strudel."

Dakota rolled his eyes. The two split, walking in different directions.

Even though James was dry by the time he entered the lobby, his disheveled appearance earned more than a few questioning glances from other guests and the staff. He stopped by Marty's stand.

The bell captain looked James up and down. "What happened to you, sir?"

"I fell in the ocean," James answered. "Is... the party we spoke about here?"

"Oh, I'm sorry, Mr. Vagus," Marty said, "but she checked out earlier today. I helped take her bags to her car."

"Damn." James ran a hand through his hair. "Do you know if she left a forwarding address or mentioned where she was going?"

"No, nothing like that, I'm afraid." Marty shook his head. "I guess you strike out this time, Mr. Vagus."

You said it, James thought. "I guess. Alright, thank you," James managed, his mind racing as he turned away from the desk and headed for his room.

Once inside, James let out his breath and flopped on the bed. He couldn't help but question the wisdom of his idea to get involved with van Heerden as an investor. His initial plan was to infiltrate the scheme, but it seemed to have backfired. Literally. Was he not convincing enough in his portrayal of a wealthy orphan? Or was his flippant remark true — van Heerden disposed of those who invested with him? Regardless, James knew he needed a new strategy, yet he was at a loss for what to do next.

When they had met, Smith told James that he probably hadn't been adopted because couples didn't want a child smarter than them. James didn't feel smart now.

That was certain. Growling in frustration, James got up and paced the floor.

"Okay, okay, I can't worry about past mistakes," he said out loud. He stopped and let out a sigh. "Alright, I'll retrace my steps. I'll check the warehouse again. Maybe I'll find something there."

James changed clothes and drove to the warehouse, parking in front with confidence. His footsteps echoed against the concrete as he left his sedan and strode toward the rear of the building with an air of authority. But when he reached the back, a sense of unease crept over him. The door was ajar and an eerie quiet wrapped around the entire structure. Cautiously, he stood to one side of the door and used his foot to push it open. The hinges creaked in proper haunted house fashion.

He held his car keys in his right fist in a hammer grip, so the keys stuck out like a knife. A handy weapon. He slid through the doorway, his back pressed against the rough concrete wall as he made his way down the short hallway. The silence inside was complete, making even his own breathing sound thunderous in comparison. The warehouse lay before him, vast and vacant. The refrigerator dolly was propped next to one wall, while the electrical cables rested coiled under the junction box.

Two doors stood open in the wall. He peeked in. The first one: the bathroom. The second opened into a small office. It was empty as was the rest of the building, but James couldn't ignore the faint chemical odor that lingered in the air. Van Heerden seemed to have pulled out of here... but what about his house?

"Next stop," James said as headed for the back door.

On the way over, James decided to try the head-on approach. He'd walk straight up to the front door. It would be intriguing to see van Heerden's response if he answered. Would there be any reaction to the failure of his hitmen? Then James planned to express interest in investing more money into the syndicate.

The sun's rays reflected off the van Heerden's crisp, white bungalow as the boring, beige sedan drove up. The driveway was deserted. James strode up to the door and knocked twice. When there was no answer, he turned around and began whistling a tune. While he did, he positioned his body in a way that blocked the doorknob from view so he could easily grab it with his hidden hand and twist it. To his surprise, the door opened — someone had not locked it. With a cheery wave and "hello", James stepped through the door as though being welcomed inside.

The bungalow appeared not only empty of van Heerden, but it felt somehow unoccupied. James got the distinct impression the property was waiting for its next tenant. The living and dining rooms were one rectangle taking up the right side of the house, with a doorway leading to the kitchen beyond. The left wall held three doors. James was about to start for the first door when a sound stopped him.

Somebody rang the doorbell.

Chapter Seven

J AMES STOOD, HEART POUNDING in his ears as the doorbell echoed through the house. For a second, he wondered if he could escape out of one of the rear windows. Or pretend he wasn't here, although his car sat parked in front, strongly suggesting somebody was home.

"Maybe it's only a door-to-door vacuum cleaner salesman," James said to himself.

The bell rang again, followed by the twisting of the doorknob. Perhaps the unknown visitor was going to let himself in like James did. He could run, but somebody else could be waiting outside.

James knew he couldn't ignore the person, or flee, so he decided to bluff his way out of this situation. Or at least try to. Whoever was at the door could be a source of more information that might be useful as well. He strode towards the door and opened it with forced nonchalance.

"Good afternoon," he said, offering the visitor on the porch his most charming smile. "How may I help you?"

The man in the doorway commanded attention with his beefy build shoehorned into a sharp, well-tailored suit. His polished cane, topped with a gleaming silver handle, added to his air of sophistication. But his broad shoulders, bulky hands, and nose that had been broken at least once hinted at a rougher side. Here stood a gentleman whose journey began in back alleys; a veneer of civility troweled over brute strength. The man's piercing gaze bore into James, unrelenting and shrewd.

"Good afternoon." The man's words slipped off his tongue like silk slipping off a spool. He had a German accent. "I am here to see Dr. van Heerden. Is he available?"

James's mind raced, trying to come up with a plausible response. He'd have to play along if he wanted to get more information.

"Ah," James said, stalling for a moment longer. He figured the simplest answer was the best one. "I'm sorry. He is not in at the moment."

"Not at home? But how unfortunate!" The man narrowed his eyes, sizing James up with a practiced ease that sent a shiver down his spine. It was clear that this wasn't his first encounter with someone who might be trying to throw him off the scent. "Could you tell me where I can find him? My business is immediate, and I have come a long way."

"That is inconvenient." James forced a sympathetic smile onto his lips. He had to think fast or risk losing control of the situation. "I'm afraid I don't know where he went." The man's steady gaze seemed to pierce through James like a dagger. "Dr. van Heerden just stepped out for a moment," he went on. "I might help. I am his assistant."

The man twirled his cane in one hand with an air of impatience. He eyed James up and down, then flashed a knowing, cold smile of comprehension. "Of course you are. Dr. van Heerden and I have an affair of great urgency to discuss."

"I'm more than qualified to handle any issues that may arise in his absence." James took a gamble and switched to German. "Does it concern the Golden Syndicate?"

The man started and looked at him, his expression mingled with suspicion and uncertainty. "It is a matter of the highest priority," the man answered in German. "It is vital."

"About the Golden Syndicate?" James tried again, in the same language.

"I know nothing about a Golden Syndicate," said the man firmly. He patted his breast pocket. "I am merely the bearer of a communication which is of the greatest importance." He repeated the words, stressing them. "The greatest importance."

"If the message is written, I will make sure he gets it." James held out his hand with the calm assurance of one who shared the dearest secrets of the doctor.

"This is only a letter of introduction. The message itself is verbal, and not something that can be delegated to an assistant," the man said. "My instructions were explicit — I must speak with him in person."

"Of course. I understand," James said, schooling his features into a look of sincere regret. He returned to English. "If you wish to wait for Dr. van Heerden, please come inside. He should be returning within a few minutes."

The man tapped his cane impatiently against the porch decking. "I suppose I have no choice, young man," he said, his tone laced with irritation, "although I cannot afford to wait around indefinitely. This matter is of the greatest importance, and I must see Dr. van Heerden as soon as he returns."

"I understand," James conceded, disguising his nerves with a relaxed smile. "It shouldn't be long."

The man hesitated for a moment, his gaze scanning the room over James' shoulder before giving a curt nod. As he stepped over the threshold, James couldn't help but note the confident and predatory grace with which the stranger moved, much like a panther stalking its prey.

"Can I offer you something to drink while you wait?" James asked, trying to play the part of a loyal assistant as he closed the front door.

"No, thank you." The man perched, rather than sat, on the edge of an armchair near the window. The tip of his cane rested between his feet, both hands clasping the top. "I prefer not to partake of refreshments when discussing matters of such importance."

James nodded in response, observing the man with a sense of relief. After all, James did not know where van Heerden kept his refreshments, and bashing about in the kitchen searching for them wouldn't add to his credibility. As the mysterious visitor glanced around the room, James' mind raced with thoughts and questions, attempting to piece together his intentions.

The silence persisted. The weight of the man's gaze returned to James, bearing down on him like a physical force.

"Please," the man said, "as Dr. van Heerden's assistant, you must have many tasks to attend to. You do not need to sit with me."

"Thank you." James tried to keep his tone light. He was walking a tightrope now, but he had no choice. He needed to know more about this visitor if it could somehow aid in his mission.

James moved to the bookcase and scanned the titles. He pulled the *Statistical Bulletin* issued by the United States Department of Agriculture and sat at the desk. Opening the publication, he noted the folded corners on the "Crop Production" and "Crop Acreage" report pages, which provided detailed statistics on those items by region and state. He extracted a pen from his pocket and pretended to be engrossed in facts such as the number of hectares under cultivation, the method by which the crop areas were divided, and the average size of the unbroken blocks of fields. He wondered what would van Heerden want with this information.

The seconds stretched into minutes, each one crawling past as James fought to maintain his feigned interest in columns of figures. All he could do was bide his time and wait for an opening to present itself.

"And you do not know when Dr. van Heerden will return?" the man asked.

"I'm afraid I don't know. I'm sorry."

More silence.

"I must stress, my business is quite urgent," the man broke the quiet, tapping his cane rhythmically against the floor. "Even more so after the recent incident in Spain."

A jolt of adrenaline surged through James, although he kept his expression neutral. What had happened in Spain, and how did it relate to van Heerden?

"Ah, of course." James turned to face the man, concealing his inner nerves with a slight nod. Here's a potential opening, a way for James to learn the information... if he could maneuver his visitor to reveal it. "Dr. van Heerden will undoubtedly want to hear your message as soon as possible."

The man inclined his head in agreement. "I am sure he will."

The shadows of the room seemed to narrow in on James, heightening the tension in the air as he studied the man before him. He couldn't allow this opportunity to slip through his fingers — he needed to learn more about this mysterious occurrence in Spain. He understood he was dancing around the open jaws of a hungry steel trap.

"By the way," the man casually asked, "How did Dr. van Heerden react to the news?"

"Well," James began, feeling a bead of sweat trickle down his temple. "Just as you expect he would."

The man's voice was almost soothing. "I've never met the man. I don't know how to expect him to act. How did he?"

James' throat went dry. He knew he was being backed into a corner, with little room left to move. His mind fired, searching for a way to escape the net that was closing in around him. He had to stay focused, and remain calm — one wrong move could cost him everything.

One of the visitor's eyebrows edged up just a bit, and a calculating glint flashed across his eyes. He leaned forward ever so slightly, his grip tightening on the silver cane. It was clear he expected an answer.

"Well, let me tell you about Dr. van Heerden." James gave a nervous chuckle, scratching the back of his head. "You know how secretive some bosses can be, right? Always playing their cards close to the chest? That's Dr. van Heerden."

"Oh? Yes, I've had employers such as that myself," the man said.

James smiled. "Then you understand."

The man nodded.

"His reaction was no reaction." James believed he had sidestepped the snare with grace.

"Ah." The man returned an understanding grin. "Then what was your opinion of the situation, then?"

James' heart pounded against his ribs. He needed to tread with care now. "Well, I wasn't informed of the incident, so I don't have one."

"You mean to tell me," the man drew out each word with sliced precision, "that you, as van Heerden's trusted 'assistant', were not told of the recent events in Spain?"

The jaws of the trap sprang shut. James stood, preferring to be on his feet if he had to fight his way out of the situation. "Well, Dr. van Heerden has been rather... preoccupied with other matters lately," he replied, forcing a casual smile. He picked up the book. "I'm sure he'll fill me in when he believes he needs to."

The stranger also got up. Perhaps he, too, expected violence. His eyes bore into James, unyielding and cold. "I am surprised. It seems quite improbable for an assistant to be so... left in the dark." His words dripped like melting ice cubes. "Especially considering the importance of the situation."

An uncomfortable silence draped the room, heavy and thick. The weight of each passing second smothered James as he racked his brain for an escape route.

The man's frosty gaze didn't waver. A slow, almost imperceptible smile crept across his lips. "While I would love to stay and discuss this matter with you further, I'm afraid I will have to take my leave, for now."

James also forced a grin. "I'm sorry your visit was in vain. I will pass along your visit to Dr. van Heerden as soon as he returns."

"See that you do," the man said coolly, his eyes never leaving James. "And remember — some secrets are best kept in the shadows. Please," he gestured towards the door with his cane, "see me out. I wouldn't wish to overstay my welcome. You must have... work to do. I am sure your duties as an assistant can be quite taxing."

"Of course." James gave a slight bow of his head.

With an unexpected burst of movement, the man lunged towards James with his cane, moving like a trained swordsman. James recoiled, but it was too late. The sharp end of the cane punctured his thigh, sending a sharp pain through his body. Gasping and stumbling back to the desk, he desperately grabbed for anything nearby to defend himself. He hurled the heavy *Statistical Bulletin* at the attacker.

The publication was swatted aside like an annoying insect, and the visitor's calculating eyes met James'. James lunged toward the man. His left hand shot out, grabbing for the polished cane in his opponent's grasp while the heel of his right hand swung towards the man's exposed neck.

The man tilted his head to the side, avoiding most of the blow and letting it graze past him. The man retaliated with an unexpected knee strike aimed at James' midsection. It connected with bruising force, knocking the wind straight out of him. James doubled over, gasping for air that wouldn't come. The man shoved James backwards. He stumbled, trying to maintain his balance before sprawling to the floor.

With an almost casual flick of his wrist, the man produced a gun from inside his jacket pocket — sleek and black — like a lethal shadow in his hand. Everything slowed down as James watched from the ground. The man's deadly weapon rested in his firm hands. For a moment, nothing was heard but silence punctuated by their heavy breathing. James felt nothing but icy dread creeping up on him.

"That was not a good idea, although I commend your courage. And your form is quite good," the man said. "However, because of the physical exertion, your heart rate is now increased. That is assisting in pumping the drug I injected faster into your brain."

"Wha... what did you...?" James managed to slur his voice just above a whisper.

"Nothing too harmful, I assure you. Just a little something to keep you... quiet. You should consider yourself fortunate," the man said, a malicious grin spreading across his features. "The needle on my cane contains a lethal dose of curare most of the time. However, I didn't know how I would have to deal with van Heerden today, so I opted for something less... permanent. Now we shall just wait until the drug takes effect. It will take a few minutes. What could we talk about to pass the time? The lovely Miami weather?"

James blinked back the sudden onslaught of dizziness that washed over him, his vision blurring at the edges like paint colors running into each other. The floor appeared to tilt, just a bit, as if mocking his attempts to hold himself together.

"There's no use fighting it. You'll only make things worse for yourself," the man said. "Just relinquish to the effects."

James crawled to the desk, braced his body against it, and struggled to his feet. He forced his legs to remain steady beneath him. The energy seeped from his limbs, replaced by a heavy, dragging weight.

"Your persistence is admirable," the man murmured, stepping closer.

James tried to throw a punch. It was wild and weak.

"Ah, I see," the man said. "It appears the drug has acted rather quickly. No matter." He reached out, gripping James's arm. "Let's get you settled, shall we? Let us make things tidy."

The room spun around James as he fought to focus. He attempted to speak, but his tongue became sluggish and uncooperative. His vision grew even more hazy. He strained against the man's hold on him, but the grip only tightened like a vise.

"I think one of those heavy chairs by the table will do," the man said, a waiter leading a diner to his seat.

James' muscles were barely keeping him on his feet. All he could do was comply, leaning on the man as his knees threatened to buckle. The man guided him towards the dining room, each step like walking through molasses. The threads of his consciousness frayed.

"This one will be fine. Sit down," the man commanded, putting James into one of the armchairs that surrounded the table. "Comfortable?"

As the last remnants of his strength evaporated, James slumped against the chair. His mind was slowing down; thoughts dripped into his brain.

"I would much enjoy seeing Dr. van Heerden's expression when he finds out what happened to his 'assistant'... or whoever you truly are. I'll ask him that when I call on him again. Sleep well," the man whispered into James' ear as darkness enveloped him, a sinister lullaby that haunted his descent toward unconsciousness.

James heard the front door open and close. From the living room came two voices... one sounded like van Heerden.

Fighting against the creeping darkness, James struggled to hang onto his senses, to push away the drug's effects as long as he could. He conjugated verbs in the languages he knew and reviewed memories from the orphanage, school, and training. Then he ran through nursery rhymes, songs, even the Mass, anything to keep his mind active. He entered a limbo, a twilight world halfway between light and shadow, a place where time slowed down, sped up, spun around, and then simply ceased to exist. Awake, but not awake. Alive, but not alive. No feeling.

A muffled groan escaped James' lips later as the drug wore off and full consciousness came back to him in gradual stages. His head throbbed without pity and could have been stuffed with wet wool. Every muscle screamed in protest, and he took a few deep breaths to clear the fog from his brain. His body felt sluggish as if held down by invisible chains. As he rejoined the land of the living, the sound of silence pressed against his ears, interrupted only by his own labored breathing.

Realization dawned that he was still in the dining room. Surrounded by early evening darkness, he was all by himself. He didn't think he had been in the thick fog for very long, maybe an hour or two at most. Van Heerden must have decided to deal with his surprise package tomorrow morning.

Either way, James didn't want to stick around to find out what that would be... other than completing the task van Heerden's goons in the motorboat failed to accomplish. James tried to move.

His wrists were bound to the chair arms with thin cords that seemed to have been cut from curtain runners. The rough material bit into his skin, leaving angry red marks that throbbed with each movement. His ankles were also bound together, making it nearly impossible for him to move. A large knot had been shoved into his mouth, filling it completely, and the cloth napkins were tied securely behind his head to keep it in place. He struggled against his restraints, but they held fast, cutting off any hope of escape.

James began to twist and turn his wrists, working the ropes against each other. Every movement sent a flare of burning shooting through his limbs, but he refused to give up.

"Come on," he urged himself, sweat beading on his brow as he strained with his bonds. "You can do this."

The seconds ticked by and the cords remained stubbornly unyielding. That obviously wasn't going to work. He decided to try an old-fashioned way and shout for help. What story to tell any rescuers later he'd figure out later.

He yelled, his voice muffled and dim. Then he listened intently. Silence. He tried again, throwing all his energy and effort into the cry. The gag sopped up the sound like it was spilled soup.

A pungent stench — like rotten eggs — crept into James' consciousness. His heart raced as he strained to identify its source, finally detecting a subtle but unmistakable hiss. His breath caught as he realized where the odor came from: through the open doorway to the kitchen. The visitor or Dr. van Heerden must have turned on the stove after securing James. Deadly fumes flowed from it and were filling the house.

Every muscle in James's body tensed as he grasped the situation. A single spark, from perhaps the pilot light in the wall heater, could set the whole place ablaze, and him with it. Or he could be asphyxiated by the gas. Whichever came first.

Chapter Eight

J AMES STRUGGLED WITH THE fabric in his mouth, twisting his head to loosen the gag. He moved his jaw back and forth while pushing against the knot with his tongue. The rotten egg smell grew stronger by the second. With one final, all-out effort, he spat out the napkins.

He had to escape before the gas overtook him and this would be the last room he occupied while alive. He fought with the ropes tying his hands to the chair, to no success. No matter how he turned and contorted his body, the tight cords on his wrists held him tight. Leaning down, he opened his mouth to grasp the knots with his teeth. The restraints mocked him by not allowing his bite to reach them by the barest amount.

"Think, Vagus, think," James told himself, the blond strands of hair clinging to his forehead as he concentrated. His eyes darted about, searching for anything that could aid in his escape.

With each passing second, the gas clawed with more persistence at his senses, a silent countdown to a choking end. James' gaze rested on the sideboard nearby. This unassuming piece of furniture now held a possible solution. A set of pristine wine glasses sat on top, catching the dim light, their stems elegant and untouched. They might just be the key to his freedom from the ropes.

With an animal-like growl, James strained as he heaved his body forward. Grunting in fierce determination, he scooted the heavy chair across the floor — dragging, hopping, sliding. Forward, sideways, forward, sideways...

Sweat broke out on his forehead, and his muscles burned with the effort as he fought to reach his target. Each grueling movement, every inch gained, notched a minor victory in his battle. He maneuvered himself next to the sideboard.

His head ached, he was dizzy, he was out of breath. He realized that was not only because of the exertion but from the gas fumes. There was no time to savor his triumph.

James stretched his neck, jaw wide open, aiming for the glinting stem of the nearest wine glass. His teeth snapped at the air, frustration wrinkling his brow. Like the knots, it remained just beyond the reach of his bite, a beckoning, taunting specter.

His eyes were drawn to the runner under the glasses. The fabric hung off the edge of the sideboard, with the glasses lined on top, like soldiers at attention. If he could pull the cloth, that would bring the goblets closer. But he also could knock them over.

He angled his head, eyes locking onto a tassel that adorned the corner of the runner. He nudged his face closer. His blond hair brushed the wood, a whisper away from success. Teeth bared like a snarling dog, he aimed for the end of the fabric. The pungent tang of gas clawed at his throat, each breath a searing challenge. James coughed.

His lungs begged for air, but he pushed the discomfort aside and focused only on his aim: retrieving a glass. He strained forward, his resolve giving him an extra boost. In a moment of victory, he bit down on the tassel. With a smooth and careful motion, he pulled on the tassel, making sure not to jostle the goblets. He couldn't risk upsetting them.

The fabric slid across polished wood with a whisper, the glasses riding precariously along the top. One shallow breath followed another, the tightening noose of gas filling his chest. He could feel it, the thickness of the air in the room, heavy with death. He let go of the runner and bit another section.

Another pull dragged his targets within reach, accompanied by the delicate tinkling of crystal against crystal. James tilted his head, aligning his mouth with the nearest goblet. His teeth closed around the smooth stem, locking onto it, the glass cool and solid in his mouth. He had his prize now, gripping it like a dog with its bone.

James arched his back, and with a swift motion, he jerked his head down. The bowl of the glass connected with the hard edge of the sideboard. A resounding crack echoed through the room as crystal splintered, pieces cascading down like icy rain.

He glanced at the result. Some glinting, jagged shards remained attached to the stem. He had done it... he created a makeshift blade.

The scent of gas was crowding around him. A cough racked his body, and he clamped his jaws tight, desperate not to lose his glass knife. James leaned forward and positioned the stem's jagged end toward the cord binding his left wrist. Twisting to find the best position, he placed the sharp edge against his bonds. He started moving his head from side to side.

The rhythmic scrape of glass on rope began sawing motions, punctuated by his labored breathing. He winced as he sometimes jabbed the back of his hand with the sharp points, drawing pinpricks of blood, but he continued to cut. Slowly, fibers frayed and parted, the strands yielding to the persistence of his emergency knife.

With each passing second, the shard did its work, cutting the ties that bound his wrist. The stem, slick and dripping with his saliva, sliced deeper, at last severing the final bit of cord that imprisoned James's left hand. The rope fell away, and his hand was his own again. James permitted himself a triumphant cry as he spat out the remnants of the wine glass.

Wasting no time, his fingers trembled as they clawed at the remaining knots on his other hand. They were stubborn, but each twist and tug brought freedom closer. At last, both hands were loose. He attacked the ropes on his ankles. As soon as they were untied, he leaped from the chair and dropped to all fours. The gas was filling the upper part of the room, so he remained on the floor, where the air was fresher. He crawled to the kitchen.

The oven gaped wide, a hissing sound spitting from the stove like an angry cat. James slammed the door closed, then turned the knobs for it and the burners to the off positions. He staggered to the window, and all but tore it open. The cool night rushed in a welcome torrent, dissipating the fumes that had begun to claim the space as their own. Pulling open the back door, he stumbled out to the backyard and collapsed on the grass. He hungrily sucked in the fresh air.

The pounding in his head subsided after a few minutes. James checked the time on his watch: 11:25 PM.

The neighboring houses were quiet and dark, their occupants likely fast asleep. His initial feelings about the house not being occupied by van Heerden any longer came back to him. He decided to return inside for a thorough check.

After an hour, James believed the house had aired out enough. He proceeded through each room systematically, checking closets and dressers for any sign of occupation. They were all empty, but some drawers were not closed all the way as though emptied in a hurry. In the kitchen, he found stocked cabinets and a full fridge. There was no evidence of a panicked departure, like forgotten belongings or unfinished meals. Everything suggested van Heerden's exit, although rushed, was not chaotic.

James ended up in the living room and flipped through each book on the shelves, hoping to find a note or message. Some books contained penciled check marks or underlined words, but they were meaningless to him. So far, his search yielded no results. Disappointed, he moved to the desk and began opening each drawer.

Despite his thorough inspection, he found nothing — not even a stray paper clip. He was about to give up when his fingers brushed against something hidden in the back of the top center drawer. He pulled it out and realized it was a piece of paper wedged between the back of the drawer and the desk.

When he read what he had discovered, he almost laughed out loud. Fast Deal Pawn, of Miami Beach, Florida, had advanced forty dollars on a "Gentleman's Gold Mühle-Glashütte Pocket Watch". The pledge had been made in the name of van Heerden.

James shook his head and slipped the loan ticket into his wallet. He chuckled. "I knew van Heerden was desperate for cash, but not that desperate."

The words of the visitor about the "incident in Spain" came back to his mind. James realized that was his next task: to find out what it was.

***

With grace and precision, Dakota maneuvered his way through the crowds filling the modern corridors of New York City's bustling Idlewild Airport. The chatter of hurried passengers and public address announcements melded into an indistinct hum, punctuated by the occasional scrap of a suitcase on the floor. Dressed in his preferred outfit of boots, jeans, denim work shirt, and corduroy jacket with a fleece collar, he brought a taste of the American West's freedom to the traveling business executives buttoned up in their three-piece suits.

It was going to be a long, tiring trip: Miami to New York, New York to London, London to Vienna. A wry smile played on Dakota's lips as his mind wandered to James. While Dakota navigated the skies, he imagined James sprawled next to the hotel pool, like a cat in a patch of sun. A cool drink, perhaps, perched on the edge of his chaise lounge.

Dakota just made the tight connection, boarding the Boeing 707 at the last call. After takeoff, the Atlantic stretched beneath him, endless and un-yielding, as the flight from New York to London cut a curving path across the night sky. Dakota's head bobbed with the gentle turbulence, but sleep remained elusive, an adversary too nimble for even him to grasp, despite the boring drone of the engines.

London was a blur, its sprawling expanse viewed through sleepy eyes as he stumbled to make his next connection. He decided someone with a bizarre and particularly nasty sense of humor designed the sprawling, maze-like Heathrow terminal. Dakota navigated through the airport as though exploring an unknown forest.

Over twenty hours after leaving Miami, Dakota's boots echoed with a rhythmic thud against the polished floors of the American Embassy in Vienna. The air was thick with the scent of waxed wood, the clacking of typewriters, the ringing of phones, and the barely perceptible buzz of conversations.

Dakota worked his way through a platoon of different staffers, passed off from one to another, until he finally stood at the desk of a secretary as she scanned his ID. Her eyes flickered with surprise at the high-security clearance level for someone only 18 years old.

"Mr. Walker, please take a seat. I need to verify this. We will arrange your meeting as soon as possible," she said with a practiced smile. She gestured toward the austere waiting area.

Dakota nodded and sat on the edge of a metal chair, his muscles involuntarily tensing as he surveyed his surroundings. This was becoming a familiar routine for him — patience disguised as calm, with every sense attuned to his environment.

After a wait that seemed as long as the trip he just finished, a man emerged from an office. He welcomed Dakota with a grin and a handshake, a signal his credentials had been approved. The official informed him that the arrangements for the meeting with the informant were in its final stages. He offered Dakota a room to rest and refresh himself, which was gratefully accepted.

After getting some sleep, Dakota left the embassy well past midnight and stepped out into the chilly Vienna night on his way to the meeting. He strode with determination through the empty streets, the city's beauty and history a silent witness to his unwavering purpose. The magnificent architecture told stories of years ago, each intricate facade a reminder of bygone days. He regretted not being more alert upon arrival; he would have loved to explore Vienna and share its glories with James.

He liked James. But as they grew closer, he couldn't help but feel conflicted. Part of him enjoyed the companionship and space that James gave him, but another part was hesitant to let anyone close after living like a lone wolf for so long. As much as he wanted a friendship, he also feared the potential loss, especially in the life they both lived now. He turned his mind back to where he was.

Vienna held a certain allure. For a city. Its attractiveness was undeniable, even to one whose heart lay in the vast openness of nature, such as Dakota. This place was so different from the wilds where he had roamed as a child when he had to...

The thought was severed, a mental door slamming shut on memories best left undisturbed. Dakota redirected his focus to the mission at hand. There was no room for the past in the life of an agent. Only the present mattered, only the relentless pursuit of what was shrouded in the shadows.

He entered Stadtpark, the extensive park in the center of the city. Wandering through the beautiful landscaping, he paused to view the gold-plated bronze statue of composer Johann Strauss. Dakota walked on, humming a few bars of "The Blue Danube" waltz to himself. His keen senses absorbed every detail — the way the leaves rustled in the gentle breeze, the soft murmurs of couples strolling hand in hand.

The night air was crisp and cool. Dakota turned down a long avenue, flanked by towering trees on either side, their branches stretching out like fingers grasping for the stars. Benches stood along the path, inviting passersby to rest and take in the vibrant foliage. The lamps that lined the way cast warm, yellow pools on the ground, creating an enchanting mood.

His sharp eyes flicked from one lamppost to another, counting under his breath, "ten, eleven, twelve..."

At fifteen, he paused. Here, beneath the gentle glow of the fifteenth lamp whose light fought back the darkness of the night, he was to rendezvous with his contact. With the ease of a panther settling into a watchful repose, Dakota lowered himself on a nearby bench. Attuned to every shift in the park's atmosphere, he waited.

Footsteps approached... hurried, furtive. Out of the corner of his eye, Dakota spotted a small man coming toward him, completely nondescript in appearance.

He scurried down the edge of the path like a rat hugging a wall.

The man halted about ten feet from the meeting place and hesitated a second. Apparently deciding, he sat upright on the bench beside Dakota. He left a careful gap between them as if the space could shield him from the dangers that nipped at his heels. The man's voice just carried over the whisper of leaves rustling in the slight breeze. "The eagle flies at dawn."

Dakota remained still, still not facing the man, his face a mask of calm. He responded with the precision of a well-rehearsed script, "And the owl at dusk."

It was done. The simple exchange of coded phrases began their clandestine meeting, binding them in a momentary alliance that vibrated with the tension.

The informant's hand trembled as he reached into the inner pocket of his jacket. His fingers fumbled before drawing out a small vial. It caught the lamp light, an ominous glint flashing against the white substance sealed within.

"Be careful, it's potent," the man whispered, a tinge of fear lacing his hushed tone. He pressed the container into Dakota's palm, its surface cool against the warmth of human skin. "This vial contains a compound strong enough to upset the global balance of power between the East and the West."

Dakota's eyes locked on the small tube, his thumb brushing the smooth glass. Its contents resembled white sawdust. "What is it? How can this —"

"It is being formulated by individual scientists in several countries, but coordinated by one. The work is almost complete," the man said, his voice a breath in the darkness. He glanced over his shoulder, a flicker of fear crossing his features visible in the lamplight. "I've heard the man behind this has now been funded by a government."

"Which one?"

"The…" The man broke off as if he picked up on something. Then, like a dried leaf blown away by the wind, he was gone — his presence absorbed by the park's sprawling expanse.

Rising from the bench, Dakota examined the glass tube, wondering why such a harmless appearing powder was dangerous. After a few moments, one end of his mouth tugged up in a half-smile. It always amused him how noisy people were when they attempted to be quiet. He stood relaxed but ready.

The man's German command came from behind him. It cut through the night air, a razor-sharp intrusion. "Hand it over."

"I don't speak German," Dakota lied.

There was an annoyed grunt from the stranger. In halting English, he gave the order again.

"If you insist," Dakota said. He spun around.

Dakota's initial strike, a swift karate chop aimed at the stranger's throat, sent the man reeling backward. The choked sound that escaped the attacker's lips echoed in the silent park, upsetting its tranquil atmosphere. The other man countered with a wild swing of his fist, aimed at Dakota's face. His movements were untamed and unpredictable, more the mark of a street fighter rather than somebody trained in combat.

Dakota deflected the assailant's punch midair by using his forearm as a barrier. His eyes never wavered from his opponent's gaze, boring in with determination, calculating his next move.

That was a roundhouse kick aimed at the man's stomach. The impact was powerful enough to send the attacker off-balance again. Their positions shifted on the gravel battlefield under Vienna's dark sky. The assailant recovered and lunged at Dakota with reckless desperation.

Dakota sidestepped just as the lunge came in his direction. He swept out one leg in a low arc towards his opponent's ankles and met no resistance as it knocked both feet out from under him. The assailant stumbled forward a few steps, flapping his arms, trying to regain his balance.

Targeting the temple on the side of the man's head, Dakota stepped in and struck with an open palm that split the night air. He yanked the man around to face him and then thrust up with the flat heel of his hand against the man's chin. The assailant's body went limp almost at once, and he collapsed onto the ground as if he were a marionette with cut strings.

Dakota scanned the area, ensuring the man had brought no friends with him. Satisfied he came alone, he dragged the unconscious form behind a dense hedge, leaves rustling softly as Dakota concealed the results of their encounter.

His heart rate slowing, Dakota realized he no longer held the sample. He must have dropped it in the fight, and it was imperative he found it before it fell into the wrong hands. He surveyed the ground, the yellow light from the lamp casting long shadows over the area.

Crouching low, Dakota's gaze cut through the dimness, the sharpness of his eyesight piercing the dark. There, among a patch of grass, a glint caught his eye — the remnants of the vial. It had been smashed open during the struggle.

Dakota made his way over to the broken container, avoiding the scattered red shards of glass. He knelt down to see if he could salvage a few grains of the sample. As he did so, he noticed the lawn surrounding the shattered container. A chill ran down his spine as he realized something was very wrong.

The tube's contents spread out and seeped into the lush green lawn. The once vibrant blades of green were turning a sickly shade of brown, shriveling up and disintegrating as he watched. The odor of decay filled the air.

The informant had warned him about the potency of this mysterious powder, but he never imagined its terrifying effects could be so quick and devastating. A chilling question dawned on Dakota — if this stuff could kill off plants in seconds, what could it do to humans?

Chapter Nine

J AMES STROLLED INTO THE Miami Public Library, following the signs to the periodicals section. Rows
of shelves filled with newspapers from all around
the globe welcomed him. The familiar scent of aging
paper and ink lingered in the air, reminding James
of the many pleasant hours he spent in the library
at the Academy. Mixed in was a faint aroma of wax
from the freshly cleaned floor tiles beneath his feet.
He went to the foreign language shelves and located
what he needed: back issues of *The* ABC, a newspaper published in Madrid.

According to van Heerden's visitor, something had
happened in that country "recently". James hoped it
meant only a few days or a week ago, so he wouldn't
have to spend too much time sifting through old
newspapers to find it. He wasn't even sure what "it" he
was looking for or what this "incident" entailed. With

any luck, he'd be in the groove and something would catch his attention when he stumbled upon it.

He pulled out the stack of folded newspapers and sat at a nearby table. Grabbing the first issue off the top, he flipped through the pages. Nothing of interest. He set to work on the next edition, then the next one, then the next one. The newspaper ink started coming off on his fingers. He hated that, frowning as he wiped off his fingertips with his handkerchief. At last, a brief report on a crop failure, buried on page 7, stopped him. James knit his brows together in concentration as he translated the text.

"Thanks to the discretion and eminent genius of Dr. Alphonso Romanos, of The Ministry of Agriculture, the farmers of the district have been spared a catastrophe much lamentable," the article began.

"Señor Don Marin Fernardey, of Gomezserracín, discovered one of his fields of wheat had died in the night and was already in a condition of rot," James said under his breath as he continued to read. The article detailed how Dr. Romanos, acting promptly, burnt the infected field to prevent the further spread of the disease.

James's gaze lingered on the words, his brain turning over the implications. He leaned back, his chair creaking slightly as his index finger tapped the newspaper in a rhythm of thought.

Van Heerden's house held a library of agricultural books filling the shelves. Was there a link between those volumes and this news story? And then there had been that visitor, the one who spoke of a message for van Heerden — the whisper of intrigue about Spain now echoing in James's mind.

What communication could have been so urgent? So vital? Was this crop failure the "incident" he referred to? What was van Heerden's connection with what happened in that European country, if there indeed was one? Or was this a bum trip?

James committed Dr. Romanos' name to memory, and replaced the stack of *The* ABC on the shelves, leaning against them while he thought. Standt had commodity price charts spread out on his hotel room desk. Were they tied in with this as well? How? James pulled some issues of *The Wall Street Journal* and went back to the table. He paged through a copy until he found the commodities reports. He laid it open before him and did the same with several additional editions.

James stared at the numbers and trends sprawled across the pages in front of him. He leaned closer to the papers as he traced the ascending graphs for wheat and corn prices with his finger, the black ink stark against the newsprint. The current price for a bushel of wheat sat at $2.00 and $1.20 for corn. But the prices for each were climbing... why?

"Because of poor weather conditions," one article cited, "and reduced crop yields." Yet some experts hinted at an undercurrent of uncertainty, something lurking like a predator hidden in a dark cave.

"Something else, something unsaid..." James repeated the words of the wary professionals. They knew something was wrong. They sensed a disturbance. No market trembled without cause, real or imaginary. Could there be a link between the destroyed wheat in one small field in Spain and the fluctuations in the prices?

He brought all the puzzle pieces back into mind. His intuition told him that there was a connection present. Everything linked. Among van Heerden, his visitor, his books, those commodity prices...

Sitting still, as though in meditation, he let all the information percolate, bang into each other, try to meld into a whole. Were these incidents just coincidences, or was there something more sinister at play? The uncertainty ate at him, but he couldn't tear himself away from the articles and their maddeningly elusive patterns. Just as James believed he was on the verge of a breakthrough, another piece of data would throw him off, collapsing his grand hypothesis. He sat there, staring off into middle distance, as he tried to make sense of the chaos.

At last, a pattern took shape. And held.

James straightened up with a whispered, "that's it... that's it."

Van Heerden's goal was to dominate the corn and wheat markets. Perhaps he was already aware of the plant disease that killed that field in Spain — James deemed it "Golden Blight" for simplicity — and the potential threat it posed to global food supply. Van Heerden had obtained knowledge about the blight, possibly from a former-Nazi associate in East or West Germany.

"No, East," James said out loud.

If an outbreak of Golden Blight occurred in East Germany, it was certain the state-controlled press wouldn't report it. Being the determined researcher he was, not to mention a political comrade of Marx, van Heerden dedicated himself to finding a solution to stop the disease. He even funded his own research through personal funds. Van Heerden blamed the UN on the phone — his attempts to get backing from various countries failed, so he turned to "investments" from others. He lured them in with promises of huge profits from increasing commodity prices that would occur once the Blight started decimating crops. He followed up by simply murdering his investors after receiving their cash. After all, in van Heerden's view, one less capitalist, the better.

Remaining true to his communist beliefs, van Heerden likely intended to offer his solution to Eastern Bloc countries instead of the Western ones. There could be no doubt this would put the Iron Curtain nations in a powerful political and financial position if the Blight were to spread through the West. The Eastern Bloc could demand whatever price they wanted for a cure for the plant disease.

This was also a strategic move that would enhance van Heerden's reputation with a particular government, which could lead to favorable relocation terms to countries like the USSR. Despite Communist nations labeling themselves as "workers' paradises," governmental leaders and favored ones enjoyed a much more luxurious lifestyle than their fellow party members did.

The empty house and warehouse showed that van Heerden had fled Miami, and perhaps the country as well. But to where? James drummed his fingers against the table. Dakota may learn something in Vienna...

An urgency was building within James now, a coiled readiness to act. He stood up, the chair scraping softly along the library floor. James shelved *The Wall Street Journal* and found a telephone booth. He dialed the familiar number, listening to the rings with an impatient tap of his foot.

A sweet, matronly voice answered. Aunt Martha was, in reality, a retired Office of Strategic Services agent now serving as a communication post for MIS-X agents. "Hello?"

"Hi Aunt Martha, it's your favorite nephew, James," he said.

"About time you called, young man," she retorted, her tone chiding, but not without affection. "Are you too involved to pick up the phone to call your old auntie?"

"I've been tied up," he replied.

"So, how are things in Miami?"

"It was hot, but now it's getting colder," James said.

"Oh, dear," Aunt Martha clucked her tongue. "That is too bad."

"Yes, isn't it? I've seen enough of Florida, so I think I'm heading off to Spain."

"Spain? What's there?"

"I'd like to see a friend of mine, Alphonso Romanos. He's a doctor now. I mean, not a real one, but he works for the government."

"I see. Young man, you could have made something of yourself if you went to college," Aunt Martha said, "but no, you wanted —"

"Aunt Martha," James groaned, "you know I was thinking of Kansas State University, but... By the way, has Dakota checked in?"

"Not yet," came the answer. "I have a mind to give him a good talking to."

"When he does, tell him his friends left town yesterday. He told you about them, didn't he?"

"Yes, he did. Oh, dear. Do you know where they went?" Aunt Martha asked.

"I have no idea. They could have just flown away." James said. "Alright, that's all from me. Keep me posted."

"Will do. Oh, and James, Uncle John sends his love," Aunt Martha added.

James grinned at the description of the serious MIS-X boss. "I'm sure he does. Bye."

As he hung up, James was confident that Aunt Martha had understood his requests to arrange an appointment, make necessary travel arrangements, and check airline flight passenger lists. He made a quick stop at the library's reference section to browse the latest catalog from Kansas State. After deciding on posing as an agronomy major, he glanced through a few more books to gain some basic knowledge on the subject. He drove to Homestead Air Force to store his surveillance equipment and shortwave radio. Aunt Martha was efficient, already having everything prepared by the time James returned to his hotel. His itinerary and tickets were waiting for him at the front desk.

The next morning found James boarding a TWA flight in New York City, his heart thrumming with an excitement that had little to do with the caffeine coursing through his veins. As the plane ascended on the last leg of his twelve-hour journey, he gazed out the window.

Despite the importance of his mission, a thrill ran through him as well. This was his first trip beyond American soil, his first taste of international intrigue. The orphanage seemed a distant memory, its walls unable to contain the world that now stretched before him.

"Let's see if you have any secrets, Dr. Romanos, of The Ministry of Agriculture," he said to the clouds below. He settled back in his seat, reviewing the facts about agronomy he had memorized in the library in case of questions from the doctor.

***

James fiddled with his watch, setting it to the current time in Madrid: 8:30 pm. He walked up to registration at the luxurious Gran Hotel Velázquez, nodding in admiration as he took in the grand lobby. The travel desk at MIS-X had good taste in hotels. He switched to Spanish as he spoke to the clerk. Just as he was given the key, the clerk slipped him a message.

Once inside his very comfortable room, he opened the envelope. As expected, it confirmed a morning appointment tomorrow for a student from Kansas State University with Dr. Alphonso Romanos. Pocketing the note, he unlocked the leather briefcase he carried. It contained a sound detection kit and various pieces of equipment he used to sweep the room for possible listening devices. He found none, then he performed a visual search just to be positive. When that came up empty, he turned in for the night.

The sun scorched the cobblestones of Madrid as James stepped out of the hotel the next morning. He was dressed as he supposed a backpacking American student would wear: sneakers, jeans, and a white button-down shirt. It was less than two miles to The Ministry of Agriculture, so James walked.

The bustling streets of Madrid overflowed with life as a constant flow of pedestrians, street vendors, and honking cars filled the thoroughfares. The air was thick with the sounds of conversation, punctuated by the occasional sound of a strolling musician's guitar. Grand historical buildings stood proudly, their baroque and neoclassical facades adorned with ornate balconies, wrought-iron railings, and intricate stonework. Scattered between these architectural marvels were modernist structures with clean lines and minimalist designs.

James couldn't help but feel drawn towards the inviting side streets that promised hidden treasures and secret corners to explore, but he knew he had to stick to his schedule and keep his appointment. He quickened his pace and entered Dr. Alphonso Romanos' office right at the appointed time.

"Welcome." Dr. Romanos, a man with silver hair and a face etched with wrinkles of someone who has spent years in the sun walking the fields, stood. "Mr. Vagus, is it?"

"Yes. Thank you for seeing me, Doctor." James shook Dr. Romanos' hand. "I am a student at Kansas State University, majoring in Agronomy. Although I'm spending my summer backpacking through Europe, sometimes I look into the agricultural situations in the countries I visit."

Dr. Romanos grinned as he sat. "Ah, the sweet time of youth. Your Spanish, by the way, is excellent." He gestured to another chair. "Please."

James nodded and took a seat. "Thank you. Sister Elena from the orphanage taught me. I was reading about that disease you discovered in the wheat field."

"Ah, yes." Dr. Romanos leaned forward over his cluttered desk. "It could have proved a most unfortunate event for our farmers."

"As someone studying the interaction of plants and soil, I found the news report interesting. Fascinating and troubling as well. I can't imagine the damage that disease would cause in Kansas." James feigned scholarly interest.

"True."

"Does a sample of the pathogen still exist? My professors would be keen to analyze it," James said. "I mean, I can't stick it in my backpack, obviously, but I can tell them where to find it."

"I am afraid there are no samples available," Dr. Romanos shook his head, regret in his eyes. "They were too volatile. They didn't survive long outside their host."

"That's too bad," James nodded, hiding his disappointment. "Might I visit the affected field? It could provide valuable insight."

Dr. Romanos shifted in his chair, then tilted back in it, gazing at James. "Why do you want to do that? The crop was burnt. You will see nothing but ashes."

James flashed his best boyish smile at Dr. Romanos. "Well, yes, I know that. But you see, if I bring some field observation notes to class, it might help me win... well, earn some extra credit with my professors."

The doctor gave a knowing grin. "I see the modern university student has changed little since my days at school."

James said nothing but returned the grin.

"The location is about an hour and a half northwest of here, in the Castilla y León region," Dr. Romanos said. "Do you have transportation?"

"No, but there will be a bus…"

"No, no. No bus. The location may be difficult to find on your own. It is outside the town of Gomezserracín. Allow me to help a future scholar in agronomy," Dr. Romanos said. "I can requisition a car and driver. One is available now. He will take you there and return you."

"I don't wish to be any trouble…"

Dr. Romanos waved one hand dismissively. "It is nothing. I would accompany you myself, but I have a meeting I must attend."

James stood and extended his hand. "Thank you for all your help."

"Think nothing of it." The doctor rose and shook James' hand, then picked up the phone. "The car is downstairs now. Let me arrange things. It's a blue Renault and will be waiting by the south entrance. The driver's name is Sergio."

"Thank you again," James said. "It was a pleasure to meet you."

"For me as well," Dr. Romanos said. "My best wishes for your future success at university."

***

The blue sedan bounced along the bumpy rural roads, and James gripped the door handle with his right hand. He tried to appear relaxed but remained ready for action at the same time. While he had struck up a friendly conversation with Sergio, his training remained on the top of his mind: always expect the unexpected, and always have a second way out. Since they traveled at a slow pace over the dusty roadways, James figured he could leap from the Renault at the first sign of danger without the chance of injury. Well, not much of a chance.

As the car glided through the gently rolling hills of the Castilla y León region, the landscape unfolded like a masterpiece painted in shades of ochre and gold. Fields, neatly divided into squares and overflowing with wheat and corn, stretched out as far as the eye could see. The warm rays of sunshine drenched the scene with a shimmering brilliance, making every detail stand out with a vivid intensity.

After a turn down a narrow lane, a stark black patch marred the vista. The car kicked up dust as it came to a halt beside the scarred earth.

"Here we are," Sergio announced.

"Wow. It looks like Armageddon hit just this spot," James observed. Not a single blade of green dared to break the charcoal surface.

"Yes," the driver muttered.

As James got out of the passenger seat, he sniffed the hot air. It carried a slight odor of decay and rot. The raspy caw of a raven broke the stillness.

Sergio stepped up next to him. "It is a place of death."

James nodded. He dropped to one knee, probing the blackened earth with one finger. Sighing, he stood and brushed off his hands. Dr. Romanos was correct. The field was now nothing but ashes. Something round and hard poked him in the back.

"Raise your hands." Sergio's voice was now cold, authoritative. "Don't make me add something else dead to this patch of dirt. I am sure you know that is a gun you feel."

"I'm embarrassed that I let you get behind me. Well, live and learn, I guess." James sighed as he put up his hands.

"Lean against the car. Spread your legs and arms," Sergio ordered.

After James complied, Sergio performed a quick pat-down search and stepped back.

"You may turn around," the driver commanded.

James did so. "Can I lower my hands?"

Sergio nodded. "At your sides." He fired a shot. James flinched. The bullet struck the ground between James' shoes, kicking up a spray of dirt. "In case you get any ideas."

James needed to stay calm, like he was trained if he wanted to survive this encounter. He pushed down his nerves to stay in control. It was a small victory, but it gave him some strength.

"Your outstanding shooting accuracy is noted," James said as he put his hands down. "Waiting for further instructions now, are we?" he probed, locking eyes with the driver. "From Dr. Romanos or Dr. van Heerden? Or both?"

"I do not know the second one."

"Ah! Dr. Romanos, then," James nodded.

The driver's tone was mocking as he spoke. "When he arrives, we will take you to a secluded area, but it won't be a pleasant ride. You will be stuffed in the trunk of the car," he said with a smirk. "The doctor has some questions for you."

"I suppose you assist the good doctor in that process."

Sergio grinned. "If he allows me, although sometimes I get too... enthusiastic. But let's wait quietly now."

James held the man's gaze, his mind racing. Dr. Romanos was mixed up with van Heerden somehow, as was this blackened field. A piece of the puzzle clicked into place, confirming his hypothesis. But before he could go on to the next step, he needed to get out of this standoff alive.

Chapter Ten

THE SUN BEAT DOWN on James and Sergio as stood next to the burnt field.

"If this is about kidnapping or robbery, I don't have much cash," James said.

"This is not about money," Sergio dismissed.

"How long do we have to wait here like this?" James asked after a pause.

Sergio shrugged. "One hour. Perhaps two."

"Mind if I have a smoke, then?" James asked, displaying a calm he didn't feel.

"With great care," grunted the burly driver, his eyes still fixed on James, gun unwavering in his grip.

James extended his left arm to the side and carefully reached into his shirt pocket with his right hand. With calculated movements, he retrieved a pack of cigarettes and shook out a specific one. Placing it between his lips, he offered the pack to Sergio. He gave it a skeptical glance before taking one for himself. James then pocketed the pack and lowered his arms back to his sides.

"Got a light?" James asked, his own hand hovering near his pocket.

"Allow me," Sergio said with a smirk as he produced a lighter from his own jacket.

James leaned closer, gripping the cigarette between his thumb and two fingers. The driver flipped open the lighter. With one fluid motion, James squeezed the cigarette, shut his eyes, and turned away. The end of the cigarette erupted with a blast of tear gas powder directed right into Sergio's face. He screamed in pain, his hands reaching for his burning eyes as he stumbled backward.

"I guess my brand is too strong." James easily disarmed Sergio by grabbing the revolver and shoving him to the ground. Wasting no time, James slipped into the driver's seat and slammed the door, dropping the gun into his lap. The engine roared to life at the twist of the key, and gravel spat from the tires as he floored the accelerator. Behind him, Sergio rolled in the ashes on the field, hands covering his face, cursing.

James' stolen Renault devoured the miles as he headed back to Madrid. In the distance, he saw another auto hurtling towards him. Its glossy black paint gleamed under the bright sunlight, perhaps a reflection of danger and death. James gripped the steering wheel tighter, his jaw clenched.

The other car flashed by. In the instant they passed, James glimpsed the passenger in the other vehicle: Dr. Romanos. The sedan executed a sharp U-turn behind James, throwing up a rooster tail of dirt, and began a pursuit.

The car gained on James, closing in on the Renault's bumper, like an approaching shark with its mouth open. James risked a glance in his rearview mirror. Dr. Romanos leaned forward over the dash, his face twisted in a furious scowl.

A slow-moving farm truck blocked the lane. James chanced a pass, narrowly avoiding a head-on collision with another truck heading in the opposite direction. The sedan pursuing him copied his movements, accelerating to keep up.

The road ahead was empty. James pushed the gas pedal all the way down, hoping that his small car could outrun the other vehicle behind him. But it seemed that Dr. Romanos was very determined to catch up.

The two vehicles approached an intersection with another country lane. James decided to turn at full speed instead of going straight. It was a risky move, but he had no other choice — he needed to lose Dr. Romanos. At the last moment, James wrenched the wheel with all his might.

Gravel flew like a disturbed flock of birds as the car's tires clawed the road and the vehicle lurched violently into the corner. The vehicle fishtailed wildly, thrashing like a beast trying to throw its rider. The steering bucked under James's grip, fighting him with every ounce of its mechanical will. His knuckles whitened as he wrestled for control, his heart pounding in his chest. Finally, he tamed the unruly machine, forcing it back onto a straight path.

He glanced at his rearview mirror. Dr. Romanos had also followed and was still hot on his trail.

James' mind was running as fast as the motor, frantically searching for a new plan. Before he thought of anything, a deafening bang shattered the air behind him. An explosion of glass flung shards flying around inside his car.

Instinctively, he picked up the gun in his lap and emptied the weapon, blindly firing back out the broken window. James knew the chances of hitting any vital were remote, but it was a last-ditch attempt to slow Romanos down. He tossed the revolver on the floor.

In a move that was more of a reflex than thought out, James grabbed the handbrake. He jerked up on the handle, slowing himself without illuminating the brake lights. The driver of the pursuing vehicle, surprised at the sudden slowdown of James' car, swerved to avoid a rear-end collision and barreled past him, the occupants' eyes wide with confusion. As the sedan passed, James released the brake and floored the pedal. He followed, now becoming the hunter, not the prey.

James' heart hammered as he closed in on Dr. Romanos' car. Adrenaline surged through his veins, giving him an almost superhuman focus and determination. Time seemed to slow down as the distance between the two vehicles lessened, his body tense with anticipation and fear.

With a primal roar, James aimed his left front bumper at their right rear one. He cranked the steering wheel, punching his car into theirs.

BAM!

The impact rocked both cars, causing them to veer off course and skid across the road. James fought to maintain control of his Renault as it spun, tires screeching against the ground.

He caught a brief glimpse of Dr. Romanos' vehicle careening off the shoulder, coming to a stop in a nearby ditch with its back end jutting up at an awkward angle and its back wheels spinning pointlessly. Smoke and steam billowed from the front of the crumpled hood. James slowed down enough to confirm that the sedan wouldn't be following him anytime soon. Dr. Romanos and his driver were trapped inside the metal husk, disoriented but alive.

James let out a whoop and pounded the steering wheel. "Yeah, baby, yeah!" He laughed with glee, wishing Dakota — and, for that matter, Smith — could have witnessed his little performance. With one last look and wave in the rearview mirror at the defeated enemy, he directed the car back toward Madrid. He abandoned it on a side street in the city, dropping the keys down a sewer grate in a final gesture of victory. He grinned as he headed to the corner.

Three hours and several slow, jostling bus trips later, he entered his hotel room. He locked the door behind him. Even though he understood he shouldn't waste the time, he took a shower anyway to rinse off what had just happened and loosen his tense muscles. Wrapping a towel around his waist, he went to the phone and placed a call. Aunt Martha's voice crackled over the line, a comforting presence.

"James? How is Spain?" Aunt Martha asked.

"It's hot... too hot for me. I think I need to leave. Immediately." James allowed himself a moment to relax in the chair.

"Oh, my!"

"Anything from Dakota yet?" He picked up a pen and began fiddling with it.

"Oh, he called, yes. I told him where his friends went. He would like you to meet you there." Aunt Martha's words were clipped, and efficient, a verbal nod to the seriousness of their trade.

"And?"

"He wants you to call him at his first 'pad', I believe that's the name your youngsters give it."

James opened the desk drawer, removing a sheet of paper. "Ready. What's the number?"

"Let's see if I can remember it," Aunt Martha sighed. "It's 8643512... or perhaps it's 22645. Oh my, I'm hopeless with numbers."

"That's all right. I've got it. I'll make sense of it," James said as he wrote down all the numerals. "Thank you, Aunt Martha. It was nice talking to you. Very informative. I'll be in contact."

"So will I," Aunt Martha said. "You're my favorite nephew. You take care, James. Bye, dear."

"You too, Aunt Martha. Goodbye." James hung up and then retrieved his wallet from his pants. He pulled out a 2-inch by three-quarters-inch pad of paper, printed with random numbers in five-digit groups. He went back to the desk, mumbling to himself, "First pad..."

At the top of the first page, there was a row of printed numbers: 73422. James divided the numbers that his Aunt Martha had given him into pairs and subtracted the first two digits on the pad from the first two of her numbers — 86 minus 73. The answer was 13, which corresponded to the thirteenth letter in the alphabet: "M." He repeated this process with each pair of numbers, ignoring carrying, until he reached the end of the message: "Madras".

"Van Heerden is in Madras, India, and Dakota is on his way," James said to himself, his fingers drumming on the desktop. "And I will be, too." He chuckled. "I'm becoming a regular member of the jet set."

Tearing the top sheet off his pad, he ripped it and the paper he used into small pieces before flushing them down the toilet. He got dressed, packed, and went down to the front desk.

"Leaving so soon, Mr. Vagus?" the clerk inquired.

"I'm afraid so. Something has come up."

The desk clerk handed James an envelope. "Oh, this just arrived for you."

"Thank you." James took and opened it. Just as he expected: plane tickets and a hotel reservation. He grinned as he tucked the envelope into his suit jacket. Good old Aunt Martha. He could count on her. One day, he'd like to actually meet her.

***

After multiple flights, spanning continents and time zones, James now believed he could now claim the title of a seasoned traveler. He flew from Madrid to Frankfurt, then onward to Delhi, before touching down in the teeming Indian port city of Madras. Despite the heat and humidity of the tropical summer causing sweat to bead on his forehead and his clothes to stick uncomfortably to his skin, James marveled at the views as he gazed out the taxi window. He hoped that no matter how much he traveled, he'd never lose the wonder of seeing new places.

The Madras roads were dense with a colorful mix of vehicles — cars honking their horns, bicycles weaving through traffic, and bullock carts plodding along. The streets were alive with activity, lined with street vendors and small shops. People packed the sidewalks — some walking purposefully with a destination in mind, others leisurely taking in their surroundings.

The buildings that rose up around him were a blend of old and modern — two or three stories tall. Some appeared as if plucked right from England, but adorned with broad colonnades, intricate archways, and round domed roofs that gave them a distinct Indian feel.

The taxi pulled up in front of The Connemara Hotel, one of the oldest in that part of the country. As James got out of the cab, he admired the expansive gardens and verandas surrounding the grand establishment. The interiors were just as luxurious as the exterior promised. After checking in at the desk, James went upstairs to Room 213 and rapped on the door. A voice responded.

"Who is it?"

"It's the Fuller Brush Man," James answered.

The door opened a crack. Dakota peered from the other side. "We don't want any."

James stuck his foot between the door and the jamb as Dakota tried to shut it. "But sir, we're running a sale on toilet brushes today."

Dakota rolled his eyes. "If you insist." He pulled the door wide.

James hauled his suitcase into the expansive room, taking in its grandeur. The high ceilings stretched up towards a whirring fan that attempted to combat the humid air. A warm breeze blew through the tall, open windows, causing their floor-length drapes to sway gently. A portable fan whirred on the nightstand. Despite the modern decor, there was an atmosphere of elegance and comfort in the rich furnishings that adorned the space.

"Very nice. Aunt Martha knows how to book excellent lodgings," James remarked.

Dakota, dressed only in a pair of white, tropic-weight pants, pointed up. "Except that doesn't make much of a difference in the temperature."

"Too hot for you?" James grinned.

"It's not the heat, it's the humidity. Smith is trying to kill me. First Miami, now here," Dakota said. "Where I grew up, it was dry heat."

James waited, wondering if Dakota was about to crack open the door to the locked room that held his colleague's childhood. It remained closed.

"I've already claimed the bed by the window and any breeze blowing through it," Dakota went on. "Oh, the room is clean. I swept it already."

James let out a relieved sigh as he removed his jacket and hung it in the closet. He traded his soggy, limp shirt for a fresh one. He left it unbuttoned, but the humidity still clung to his skin like a sauna. "So, what's the deal? What happened in the old country?" he asked, plopping down on his bed.

"Maybe the old country to you, but not to me." Dakota went to an ice bucket and loaded up a tumbler, then poured some water from a pitcher. He sat on the other bed. Between swallows of water, he summed up his experience in Vienna.

"The informant gave you a vial which contained something that, when it broke, killed the grass on contact," James clarified.

"Yes. The grass turned black, and there was a smell of decay," Dakota said.

"Where did your informant obtain the sample?"

"He didn't say. He got spooked and ran." Dakota took another long drink.

James was quiet for a second. "Did he seem like he was a chemist? Like Bridgers?"

Dakota snorted. "Oh, come on, man, get real. The guy didn't present a union card or dress in a lab coat. But I would say he appeared to be educated. Certainly not like your average thug. Beyond that, he's a mystery. And now our sharing time continues. James, would you like to contribute something?"

James related what happened in Miami, his visit to the empty warehouse, and the occurrence at van Heerden's house.

"You cut yourself free with a wine goblet?" Dakota asked, one eyebrow arched.

"A broken one, yes."

Dakota raised his glass in a toast. "Even Smith would be impressed by that."

James grinned, not without some pride. "Maybe I'll get the hang of this spy business after all."

"So, where do we stand now?" Dakota went to refill his glass.

"Your capture and escape from the warehouse probably spooked van Heerden." James pointed to the pitcher. "Could you pour me one, too, please?"

Dakota imitated a bartender at a cheap bar. "Ya want on the rocks or straight up, pal?"

"On the rocks."

Dakota nodded and dumped some ice cubes in the other tumbler and filled it with water.

"So van Heerden pulled out of Miami. He must have been out arranging that when I called at his house." James went on as he took the drink Dakota held out. "Cheers." They clinked glasses. "It just so happened a mysterious messenger popped in for a chat at the same time. I'll wager he bore the news of some government funding."

"Confirming what the informant told me in Vienna." Dakota sat back on his bed. "Although the contact fled before he let me know which one had given backing."

James nodded. "Too bad. The fact van Heerden's visitor claimed he had 'vital information' and mentioned the incident in Spain suggests he was bringing the good word about finances to the doctor. At least to me, it does. I mean, why else would he insist on talking to van Heerden in person? Because he had a message that couldn't be trusted to be delivered any other way."

"I'll buy that. You said the guy spoke German," Dakota said. "Do you think he was from the Stasi?"

"He may have been from the East German secret police, but I don't know. Just having an accent and speaking German isn't enough evidence, though." James shrugged. "He might have been a freelance courier, hired for a job. Just before the drug made me go nighty-night, I heard two voices talking."

"Van Heerden one of them?"

James nodded. "I think so. After I got free, I searched the house. Van Heerden had already split by then."

"He must have rented the warehouse and house under phony names. That's why Aunt Martha was able to find his real name on the airline manifest. The separate identities between the renters and flyers couldn't be connected by authorities." Dakota drained the last of his water and put the tumbler down on the nightstand with a thunk. "Okay. Then off you went to Spain."

"It was a quick visit." James told Dakota of his interview with Dr. Romanos and what happened in the decimated field.

"Damn, it's humid." Dakota flopped back on the bed, propping himself up by his elbows. "We're still left in the dark about what van Heerden's game is. Other than he's playing in the international arena."

"Well, I thought I knew the reason," James said.

"Thought?"

James explained his theory about van Heerden trying to corner the wheat and corn markets.

Dakota nodded. "That sounds plausible..."

"Yeah. But the happenings in Vienna and Madrid blew it out of the water," James grumbled.

Dakota sat up. "How does that change your idea?"

"The field in Spain also had a slight odor of decay. And I'll bet it looked the same way as that grass in Vienna before it was torched," James said. "Dr. Romanos told me that the Golden Blight — that's what I've named it — couldn't survive outside its host. But you were provided a living sample."

Dakota shrugged. "Obviously, Romanos lied to you."

"But why?" James got up in frustration. He returned his glass to the tray.

"To keep the whole Blight story secret, of course," Dakota said. "He didn't want a random college student from Kansas blabbing about it all over Europe. Especially not to his future agriculture professors, who would want to contact the doctor to study the disease. Spain is a dictatorship under General Franco, so the news is tightly controlled. The government could make the entire incident disappear, or not appear dangerous in print."

"I suppose Romanos could be a supporter of Franco, and toe the party line, but I think he is in van Heerden's employ. Or at least bribed by him." James paced the room, running his fingers through his hair. "Perhaps the appearance of the Blight in that Spanish field provided an opportunity for van Heerden to test his treatment. A real-life experiment."

"And it failed," Dakota offered. "That's why the crop was burned. To hide the evidence of both the Blight and the ineffective treatment."

"That's a potential explanation, but..." James slowly nodded, then additional possibilities began to push into his brain. An unsettling thought about what could be van Heerden's scheme took shape. And it was horrible. "No, I'm wrong... completely wrong. I can't believe I never saw it before." He slapped his forehead in frustration and disbelief. "Van Heerden isn't trying to corner the global grain market! How could I have been so stupid?"

"Do you want an answer to that?" Dakota asked.

"No." James sat on the bed and met Dakota's eyes. "Van Heerden isn't trying to develop a way to stop the disease, but *use* it. The Golden Blight is a biological weapon."

Chapter Eleven

"A BIOLOGICAL WEAPON!" DAKOTA'S usual stoic expression slipped as he jumped to his feet. "Some kind of contact poison? Or is it dumped in the water supply?"

James shook his head. "I don't think it's aimed at humans... I mean, not directly. No, this is warfare is directed toward crops."

"Crops?"

"Think about it." James stood and paced the floor. "The Golden Blight isn't the same as dropping a nuclear bomb. Buildings aren't flattened and radiation isn't spewed everywhere. But what if the Western powers' food sources fail... " He shook his head. "The Blight would be like a scythe wielded by the Reds, slicing the fields down to the dirt."

Dakota nodded and sat again. "Starvation doesn't care about borders. Destruction of the wheat crop would cripple a country's economy, cause instability and create dependency on the only source of the grain: the Eastern Bloc. They would have won the Cold War without firing a shot." He thought for a moment. "Do you think it is possible to guard the fields by local action?"

James shook his head. "I doubt it. That would mean the mobilization of millions to surround all the wheat farms throughout the Western world. Not to mention the Golden Blight could be delivered by a hundred different methods. Plus, we don't even know how the Blight works. Does it attack the plant, the soil, or both?" His gaze fixed on something unseen as he thought about the potential aftermath. "And if the Blight poisons the ground for some amount of time, we could be talking about years before a viable crop can grow again. Or until a hybrid strain of wheat is developed, that would be resistant to the disease."

"Meaning we could be looking at a decade of rationing and food shortages, at least," Dakota said. "The US might have enough reserves for a year or two, but they won't last forever."

"Meanwhile," James picked up the thread, "the Eastern Bloc sells their surplus at premium prices."

"And world power shifts," Dakota concluded, the finality of the statement hanging between them like a dark prophecy. "The Cold War doesn't end with the nuclear blast everybody fears, but with empty bowls."

He said in a low voice, "Wow, that's heavy." A second later, he went on, his fingers tapping a staccato rhythm against the bedspread. "Spain must have been only a testing ground. A proof of concept for something far more insidious. The country may be a dictatorship, but it is not aligned with Communist ones. Maybe that's why it was picked."

Their eyes met in a tense moment as they both grappled with the weight of the plot. The silence stretched until James spoke up, breaking the tension between them. "The only thing to do is to catch van Heerden and stifle the scheme at its source. And van Heerden — why is he here, in Madras?"

"Plausible deniability," Dakota said. "No one wants a repeat of the Cuban Missile Crisis. Too many nervous fingers on too many nuclear triggers."

"Possible," James continued, "and besides, van Heerden's backers wouldn't want this kind of operation on their home turf. An accidental release of the Blight would be catastrophic."

"Simple self-preservation," Dakota said. "Whatever government is backing it, they're playing a dangerous game from a distance, using van Heerden as their surrogate. A willing surrogate."

"And we need to upset the board," James stated.

"Time to turn this over to the CIA?" Dakota asked.

James nodded. "I'll call Aunt Martha for the information."

A quick conversation yielded the coded address of their local contact. The pair decoded and memorized it before flushing their notes down the toilet. After getting dressed, they headed down to the lobby to make their way to the contact's house. They had just stepped off the elevator when Dakota put his arm out and stopped James.

"Wait," Dakota's voice cut through the murmurs of the evening crowd. His eyes were fixed on a figure across the grand space. Hilda Glaum, her blond hair cascading over the shoulders of her crimson dress, stood by the concierge desk, unaware she was being watched.

"Perhaps it's time for a reunion," James said in a hushed tone. Without any further words, Dakota disappeared into the other guests as if he were a ghost. James strode forward, each step deliberate, closing the distance between himself and Hilda. She turned, her surprise flickering like a candle flame before she masked it with a cool smile.

"Miss Glaum," James began, his voice steady. "I believe the line for occasions like this is 'fancy seeing you here.'"

"Mr. Vagus," she replied smoothly, regaining her composure as swiftly as she had lost it. "To what do I owe the pleasure?"

"Coincidence, Miss Glaum. A simple coincidence," James said, his gaze unwavering. "It happens, doesn't it?"

Her eyes narrowed slightly, assessing him. "I'm afraid I'm not a believer. How did you find out I was here? Did fate provide you with that information as well?"

"Bribes can be most useful." James gave a half-smile. "Everybody has a price."

"Including you?"

James nodded.

Hilda chuckled. "Am I to believe I was what brought you to Madras? I'm quite flattered."

"You may not be. I only wish to keep an eye on my investment. Fifty thousand dollars is rather a large sum for me," James said.

"Dr. van Heerden will pay your dividends," Hilda said.

"I hope so, but I must admit, I have my doubts." James gave a slight shrug. He watched her carefully as he continued. "You see, after our little exchange of cash at the restaurant, somebody attempted to machine gun me the next day while I was on an ocean fishing trip."

"Most unfortunate." Her voice held no emotion. "And you believe Dr. van Heerden was behind that?"

"Seems logical. I'm sure the gentlemen in the other boat weren't after the marlin I caught." James leaned in closer, the scent of her perfume unable to mask the underlying tension. "You're a confidant of Dr. van Heerden's, aren't you? You know where he is."

"I shall answer no questions." Her lips pressed into a thin line.

"That won't change the fact that you put me in touch with him in the first place." James' voice was low and measured. "And after our dinner meeting, which you arranged, someone tried to turn me into fish food."

"None of that can be proven. It's your word against ours." She emphasized the plural.

"No? I have his signed receipt," he reminded her.

Hilda eyed him for a long minute before speaking. Her question came out almost as an accusation. "Who are you, Mr. Vagus?"

"An orphan with money. One who wants even more, to maintain the lifestyle to which I have become ac-customed." James winked, and tacked on in a conspir-atorial tone, "Of course, I might be a secret agent."

She seemed to consider the idea for a moment, then trilled a laugh and stepped closer to him. "They must be recruiting young. And very handsome. You may be too young to drink, but old enough for..." Gazing into his eyes, her fingers grazed along the edge of his jaw-line, then traced his lips. She whispered seductively. "Why don't we get out of this heavy traffic? We can discuss this matter in private... let's say, in my room."

"That is a delightful proposition," James said, "but I value my safety. Public places seem safer, although that didn't help Herr Standt, did it?"

"No, that is true." Hilda gestured toward the French doors. "Then may I suggest the veranda as a compromise? Away from these people in the lobby, but still in the open?"

James nodded in agreement and the two strolled outside. The day's oppressive heat had given way to a refreshing coolness, carried by a gentle breeze that rustled through their hair. They turned the corner of the building and then stopped. "What do you know about van Heerden's scheme?"

She regarded him warily. "I'm not going to discuss my business — or his — and I don't care what you threaten me with."

"Oh, I will do more than threaten you," James said, his smile tight. "But understand this: unless you give me satisfactory answers, I'll see to it that both you and Dr. van Heerden end up behind bars. Tonight."

"You can't do that," she dismissed.

"Don't be too sure. Let's just say I have connections," James hinted. "After all, wealth has its privileges."

Hilda regarded him with cold eyes, seemingly making unthinking calculations. "Then what do you want?"

"Your friend, Dr. van Heerden's, location." James delivered the demand in a calm, matter-of-fact voice.

Hilda looked down, then gave him a coy glance out of the corner of her eyes. She opened a button on his shirt and slipped her fingers inside. "You are asking quite a bit, Mr. Vagus."

James sighed as he removed her hand. "This is getting tedious. I'm not going to pretend and dance around anymore. The game is over, Miss Glaum — I know all about the Golden Syndicate. And that includes its goal."

Hilda's hand flew to her mouth, her poise displaying a few cracks. "What do you mean?"

"Mean? How about this: Van Heerden is playing a dangerous business against the Western powers. We'll just leave it there. I wish to speak with him — quietly, without fuss."

"About what?" she pressed.

"The size of my dividends from the Syndicate," James answered.

"What's in it for me?" Hilda bluntly asked after a pause.

"If you take me to van Heerden, I may be... 'persuaded' to forget about your role in this sorry situation. If it should come to that."

A smile spread on Hilda's lips. She spoke with a touch of admiration. "Why Mr. Vagus, I'm surprised. You're nothing more than a common little black-mailer."

"A blackmailer, perhaps," James allowed, "but I certainly hope not common."

Hilda retreated a few steps. James detected that movement and instinctively took a step back as well. A dagger whizzed between them and plunged into the wall, just barely missing James' cheek. Proud he didn't flinch this time and remained composed, he wrenched the weapon out of the wood before grabbing onto Hilda's wrist with his other hand. The bushes nearby rustled and snapped as a struggle took place behind them, but soon fell silent.

James held the knife up and pulled Hilda to him. His voice was tinged with anger. "This sort of thing has been occurring to me at an alarming rate. It's beginning to tick me off."

Hilda winced under James' grip. "Let go. You're hurting me."

"I'm afraid I can no longer offer to forget your in-volvement in this affair. That is now off the table," James said in even tones. "You have a simple choice. One, take me to van Heerden, or two, we go to the hotel manager about this little incident, and I press charges. They may not lead anywhere, true, but they will most definitely be inconvenient. At least one night in the local jail."

Hilda shot him a venomous look. "You call that a choice?"

James nodded. "Yes, if not an especially pleasant one."

Hilda was silent for a minute. "Very well. I will take you to him."

***

Hilda spoke not a word during the journey, and James wasn't inclined toward conversation. He sat in the back of the taxi, gripping the dagger under his jacket. At George Town, a commercial area filled with numerous warehouses, the cab was dismissed.

"We cannot go all the way by car. We will need to walk," Hilda said. "This way."

James slipped the blade into his belt. He and Hilda went on in silence, turning from the main road, plunging into a labyrinth of streets. It seemed to James he had passed in one step from one of the best-class quarters of Madras to one that was devoted to the needs of commerce.

"The location is at the end of this street," Hilda said. They came to what appeared to be a stable yard. There was a blank wall with one door and a pair of gates.

Hilda took a key from her bag, opened the small door, and stepped in, and James followed. They stood in an area littered with casks. On two sides of the yard ran low-roofed buildings which could have been used as stables. She locked the door behind her, walked across the space to the corner, and unlocked another door.

"There are fourteen steps down," she said. "Have you a light of any kind?"

James took a pencil flashlight from his pocket. "Always be prepared."

"Give it to me," she directed. "I will lead the way. Watch your step."

"Remember, Miss Glaum, I'm not playing around anymore," James warned.

"Of course, Mr. Vagus," Hilda said. "It's your show."

The two stepped through the door into a small vestibule.

"What is this place?" James asked after she had locked the door.

"It used to be a wine merchant's," Hilda said, the bored tour guide. "We have the cellars."

"We?" James repeated.

Without responding, she gestured for James to follow her as they descended the stairs. The only illumination came from the flashlight she gripped in her hand. At the end of the staircase, there was a short hallway that led to another shut door. She unlocked it. The two continued down the corridor until they reached a third door.

"Another one? What is this place, Fort Knox?" he said as a flashlight beam hit a steel door a dozen paces ahead. He brushed past Hilda and stepped closer to the door to inspect it.

"It is the last one," she said. Suddenly, the light went out. "There's something wrong with your flashlight," she said from the blackness, "but I can find the lock."

James heard footsteps, the slide of a bolt, but realize what had happened. The door behind him slammed shout. He spun around to face it. The light was flashed on him, level with his eyes.

"You can't see me," said Hilda's mocking voice, "I'm looking at you through the little spy-hole. Did you see the spy-hole, clever Mr. Vagus? And I am on the other side of the door." She laughed. "Are you going to arrest the doctor tonight? Are you going to discover van Heerden's secret — eh? That is what you want, isn't it? Take over the scheme yourself, my common little blackmailer."

"Hilda," James said, "you will be sensible and open that door. You don't think I came here alone. I was shadowed all the way."

Another short, sharp laugh. "You lie," she said in a cool tone. "Why do you think I dismissed the cab and made you walk? There was nobody behind us. I checked. Oh, young, naïve Mr. Vagus! You may think you are intelligent, but you are playing way out of your league."

James almost laughed out loud. You don't know Dakota, lady, he thought. The snap of the shutter closing echoed in the room. From outside the door, he heard a light patter of feet. Hilda must be on her way back to tell the doctor of her lucky catch.

"So that's that," James said.

Reaching into his pocket, he pulled out a match and struck it. He walked back to the other door to examine it. It was sheathed with iron. He tapped the brick walls with his fingers but found nothing to encourage him. The floor was solid. The low roof of the passage was vaulted and cased with stone. He blew out the match. He lit another and checked the door he came through. The building was old, and there was a gap between the door and the frame. The soft brass glimmer of a bolt reflected through the crack in the flickering flame. James dropped the match to the ground.

"Always be prepared," he said to himself with a smile. He reached into his coat pocket and retrieved a fat fountain pen. After unscrewing it, he extracted a straight metal rod. Running his fingers along the rod, he felt indents at one end. He bent that part of the rod down, then repeated the process at the other end. Slipping the bent rod into his pocket, he reached again for his pen, this time removing a saw blade. He sprung the blade into the metal rod, creating a miniature hacksaw. With his fingertips, he located the gap in the doorway and slipped the blade through. He started sawing at the bolt.

***

Dakota doused his flashlight and crouched behind the crate at the hurried click-click-click of approaching high-heeled shoes. When the sound had swept past, he peeked out. The silhouette of a woman, framed by the bouncing, circular output of a flashlight she held, disappeared up the stairs. Dakota stood at the echo of a closing door. Switching on his flashlight, he continued down the hallway.

Another door blocked his path, and he twisted the knob. Locked. He pulled the lock pick knife out of his pocket, dropped to one knee, and wedged the flashlight between the stones in the wall, more or less pointing the beam at the lock. He began to work.

"Knock, knock." James' voice came from the other side of the door.

Dakota grinned. "Who's there?"

"Pick."

"Pick who?"

"Pick up the pace or we'll be here all night."

Dakota groaned. "Spare me." Some more scrapes came from the lock as he fiddled with it. "Give me a second. You're better at this breaking-and-entering stuff than me." A click came. "There. Got it."

The door swung open and his flashlight fell on James, arms crossed and leaning against the wall. "What took you so long?"

"Couldn't find a parking place."

"I'm glad you're here. I wasn't looking forward to sawing my way through that door." James replaced his miniature hacksaw in his pocket and flexed his fingers. "Did you see Hilda?"

Dakota nodded. "She scampered past me on her way out." He gestured in the direction. "I was behind a crate at the time."

"She must be happily skipping her way to van Heerden to report about her catch of the day."

Dakota nodded as he stowed his lock pick pocket knife. "It's like a labyrinth down here." He flashed his light around the corridor. "We are not alone in this building."

"Hilda said van Heerden was using the cellars." James jerked his head down the corridor, toward the open arch at the far end.

"Let's dig it." Dakota aimed his flashlight down the hallway in that direction.

James withdrew the dagger from his belt and held it up. "By the way, who was the owner of this little beauty?"

"Local hire. Nobody important." Dakota led the way down the passage toward the opening.

The archway opened onto six sturdy stone steps leading down to a small room. It was sparse, furnished with only a sink, two camp beds — remnants from what looked like part of an ambulance — and a dilapidated chair. Evidence of discarded first-aid equipment lay scattered about the room. Odd bits and pieces of bandages littered the floor, while empty medicine bottles and a shattered glass measure rested on the shelf above the sink.

James leaned toward Dakota. "This may have been used as an air raid shelter during the war. Some kind of medical station."

Dakota nodded as he shone his flashlight around the room. On the opposite wall, facing the stairs, stood another door, bolted shut from their side. The two went up to it. Dakota grasped the knob and slid the heavy lock back without noise. Quickly extinguishing his flashlight, he turned the handle and pushed the door open.

The room beyond was cloaked in complete darkness. After taking a few cautious steps inside, he whispered to James to follow. As he did so, Dakota flicked his light back on to reveal a disused space. Shelves lined the walls, holding nothing but dust and cobwebs. A handful of old wine bins huddled in one corner, their contents long gone. James tapped Dakota on the shoulder and pointed to yet another door tucked away in the far corner.

"How many doors are in this place?" Dakota grumbled under his breath.

Padding over to the door, the teen agent leaned against it and placed one ear on the wood. From the other side came the low murmurer of voices and clinking of glassware. He looked at James and nodded, making a "talking" sign with one hand. Pocketing the flashlight, he took hold of the doorknob. With a deep breath and a glance toward James, he slowly turned the rusted handle and cracked the door open.

A blinding green light seeped through the small opening, causing him to squint. He didn't dare open the door any further, afraid of being spotted from the other side. The sound of muffled voices and the occasional clink of glass against glass grew louder, along with the shuff-shuff-shuff of slippered feet crossing the floor.

After a long minute, Dakota softly closed the door. He put his lips next to James' ear and whispered. "We've hit the mother lode."

Chapter Twelve

J AMES PULLED THE DOOR open a quarter of an inch and glued his eye to the crack. At this angle, he could only see one of the walls of some big vault. Also visible was the end of a long mercury vapor lamp which stood in one of the cornices, supplying the ghastly, bluish-green light. Then he spotted something that could be useful.

Against the wall was a high shadow which even the overhead fixture did not wholly wash out. It was an irregular shape, such as a stack of boxes might make. It occurred to him that perhaps beyond his range of vision there was a barricade of cases which hid the door from the rest of the room. He closed the door and whispered his findings to Dakota.

"Looks like an invitation," Dakota said.

"Let's take it," James replied.

With a quick, confident motion, James swung open the door and stepped through, closely followed by

Dakota, who shut the door softly behind them. As James hoped, they found themselves in a small, makeshift lobby area created by a towering stack of crates arranged in an "L" shape. The boxes were neatly organized, with two larger ones at the corner that seemed to hold everything together. The rest were smaller containers roughly ten inches square, forming a solid barrier that reached about two feet from the ceiling.

A stepladder was close by, most likely used by the person in charge of organizing this stack. James quietly lifted it, placed it against a large crate, and climbed up. He peeked over the top.

The chamber's vaulted roof, supported by six sturdy stone pillars, towered above. The roof also held mercury lamps, casting an unhealthy hue over the room. But it was not just those lights that glowed with light. Suspended over two rows of benches were more lamps, their shades made of glistening mica. Each bench was occupied by figures dressed in white jumpsuits, their faces concealed behind eerie rubber masks and their hands by gloves.

In front of every man sat a small, delicate microscope, accompanied by a set of precise balances and an orderly rack filled with shallow porcelain trays. Despite the manner of their work, their eyesight seemed to be spared from harm, as they wore no protective coverings over the lenses of their masks. The hoods covered their heads completely, so not even a trace of hair was visible. This only added to the strange and animal-like appearance of the men.

James' gaze scanned the workbenches, taking in every detail with fascination. Some workers were deeply engrossed in apparently conducting tests, their focus unwavering on their microscopes. Others were examining the substance in their porcelain trays, using slender glass rods to stir and transfer tiny samples onto a slide for closer inspection. The atmosphere was thick with concentration and diligence as the group worked, with everyone immersed in their own meticulous task. James picked up on a faint musty odor of decay, the same one from the Spanish field, permeating the air.

Some men carefully filled test tubes with the substances from Petri dishes and sealed them. The vials were fragile, and James saw three break in the workers' hands. Every workstation held approximately one hundred containers and had a gas jet available for melting wax.

The tasks were performed in silence. James watched for several minutes as they worked, placing the full tubes in a small box. Layering each delicate vial with soft cotton, they packed the boxes and closed them. Then, a worker would carry them out of the room and into another, presumably for storage of the final product. Despite the strong chemical smell lingering in the air, some removed their masks once they left their stations. From his limited view, James could tell that this was indeed a factory.

James got down and whispered to Dakota. "They may be making the Golden Blight. I need to get in and be certain before we take action... and I want to get a sample."

Dakota nudged James, jerking his head towards a jumble of clothes peeking out from some cardboard boxes nearest the wall. The pile contained the same gear worn by those at the workbenches.

It seemed like someone had hidden them there, and not very well. James eyed the clothing for a second, then turned back to Dakota. He flashed a smile and nodded in agreement. Without hesitation, he took off his coat and donned the overalls, mask, and gloves. He shuffled around the stack and took up an empty position at the end of one table. None of the other workers paid any attention to him. Glancing out of the corner of his eyes, he copied the actions of the others. A familiar voice came from the other room.

"He's in the old passage, eh?" said van Heerden, the anger in his voice barely controlled. "That young man is more trouble than the money I received from him. Well, there's no reason he should get out — alive."

Van Heerden and Hilda entered the laboratory.

"I didn't think he would," said Hilda.

"He wasn't followed — you saw nobody outside?" van Heerden asked.

"He said he was, but that was a sham. I looked and discovered no one. He's working on his own." Hilda smiled in triumph. "What are you going to do with him?"

"Deal with him, but correctly this time," said van Heerden in a bland tone, "but he may have a gun. We can't afford the noise or upsetting them." He waved one hand toward the workers and Hilda nodded. Van Heerden thought for a moment. "Wait until the men have gone. I let them go at three — a few at a time. If that requires half an hour, so be it. Mr. Vagus can bide his time. He's safe enough where he is."

The pair strolled over to a nearby bench. The worker at that station lifted his mask, revealing an aged face with a toothless grin aimed at van Heerden. "Buona sera, Signor Dottore," he greeted in Italian. "Science is lengthy while life is brief, signor." He chuckled and put his mask back on before resuming his work. He paid no more attention to van Heerden and Hilda as if they were invisible to him.

"A little mad, old Castelli," said van Heerden to Hilda after they walked a little farther down the workbench. "That's his one little piece. He lost his wife and two daughters in the Messina earthquake. I picked him up cheap. He's a useful chemist, despite the oddness."

Van Heerden and Hilda moved from bench to bench. The men were departing now. One by one, they covered their instruments and their trays, slipped off their masks, overalls, and disappeared through the door to the other room. James assumed the exit from the cellars was there as well. Soon James was alone, sitting and peering through the eye-piece of his microscope.

"That's our friend Bridgers," said van Heerden to Hilda. "I am sure he's all lit up with the alkaloid of Enythroxylon Coca. Well, Bridgers, nearly finished?"

"Huh!" James grunted without turning.

Van Heerden shrugged his shoulders. "We must let him finish what he's doing. He is quite oblivious to anybody when he has these fits of industry." He watched James work for a moment, then leaned in for a closer look. "Wait a minute... that's incorrect. Bridgers wouldn't make that type of mistake..." He grabbed James by the shoulder and spun him around. "Who are you?"

James removed his hood as he stood. He remembered he still had the dagger... but it was unavailable to him, since it was in his belt, under the overalls. He would have to play it cool and hope for Dakota to do something. So he leaned against the edge of the bench. "I was never any good in chemistry class."

Hilda gasped. "You! How did you get out?"

James shrugged. "Magicians never divulge the secrets behind their tricks."

Van Heerden pulled a revolver from one of his coat pockets. "I will be interested to see your trick at dodging a bullet."

"So will I. However, that is all beside the point," James said. "Dr. van Heerden, what have you to say about my having you arrested on a conspiracy charge?"

Van Heerden flashed a contemptuous smile. "American brave talk! What do I have to say? There are many things I can say. Ignoring your current situation, I would say you have no authority to arrest anybody. Even if you escaped again, you're not an officer of the law, but only an amateur."

"American, yes... but amateur, no," said James calmly. "And I guess I can take you to the police first and figure the authority out after."

"Authority? Whose authority?" Van Heerden said with scorn.

"He says he's a secret agent." Hilda hurled the words at him.

Van Heerden looked James up and down, then burst into laughter. "The West truly must be absolutely corrupt if they are sending youth out for such dangerous jobs."

"Well, at least we're not as bad as Hitler's Volkssturm... A militia made up of sorry old men and children, expected to stop the Russian army in Berlin." James mocked.

With a roar, Van Heerden backhanded James across the face. After a second, he calmed down and smiled. "To continue playing your little game... with your imaginary 'authorities'... On what charge would I be charged?"

"There is nothing secret about this place, except Dr. van Heerden's association with it," Hilda said. "A professional man is debarred from mixing in commercial affairs. Is it a crime to run a — " She looked to van Heerden for clarification.

"A germicide factory," said van Heerden promptly. Hilda nodded.

"Suppose if I know the actual purpose of this laboratory?" asked James.

"Carry that kind of story to the police and see what steps they will take," said van Heerden with scorn. "I will save you the effort. None."

"That is open to debate," James said, "but what interests me just now is what I've named the Golden Blight. And I'm looking for you to supply a few of the missing pages. I think you'll do it."

The doctor chuckled, a gleam of malicious amusement in his eyes. "Your fantasies would exasperate me, but for your evident sincerity."

"I tell you what, van Heerden, I'm going to call your bluff. I will place this factory in the hands of the police, and I'm going to bring in the greatest scientists in America, England, and France, the entire free world. I will prove the charge I will make against you on the strength of this!" James swept his hand around the laboratory. "Everybody, even the skeptical, will know the hell you are preparing for them."

"What a lovely little speech, Mr. Vagus. I am touched by your eloquence. Nevertheless, we have wasted enough time with our pointless little chat. I will ring down the curtain on your performance... and your life," van Heerden said. "Your next appearance will be floating face down in the Bay of Bengal. By the way, where is Bridgers? Those are his work clothes."

"I have no idea," James shrugged. "I found them."

Behind the boxes, Dakota coiled himself tightly, waiting for an opportunity to rush van Heerden. A slight noise came from in back of him. He spun around to face Bridgers. The chemist's eyes were dilated.

"You! You were in Miami!" Bridgers pointed at Dakota.

Bridgers charged at Dakota. The two crashed through the stack of cardboard boxes and hit the floor, grappling. Seizing the distraction, James' left fist shot out like a cobra striking its prey, clipping Hilda's chin. At the same time, his right hand lashed out to ensnare van Heerden's gun-wielding hand.

A surprised grimace spread across Hilda's face as she stumbled back from the unexpected blow. Van Heerden's fingers clenched around the handle of his revolver as he attempted to wrench it free as James now gripped it with both his hands.

Grunting like two animals, James and van Heerden struggled. James gave a swift knee jab to van Heerden's gut, then pushed van Heerden against a workbench. The impact sent it teetering precariously on its legs, causing the microscope perched at its edge to wobble.

The bench tilted, and the microscope wavered before tumbling to break apart onto the cold tile floor. Test tubes and porcelain trays followed next, clattering and crashing as the table overturned. Their contents pooled together and shards of glass flew, making delicate tinkling sounds.

Dakota broke free from Bridgers' hold and scrambled to his feet. He held his stance as the chemist stood. Bridgers lunged forward again, aiming a blow at Dakota's face. But Dakota was ready for it this time. He feinted to the right before pivoting on his heel and dodging to the left. Dakota retaliated with a quick jab to Bridgers' side, followed by a firm slug on Bridgers' jaw.

The blow caused no reaction. Bridgers charged once more. Dakota sidestepped and thrust his elbow into Bridgers' stomach, causing the man to double over. Staggering from the force of the punch, he crashed into a pile of cardboard boxes with a loud thud. Bridgers got up again, he and Dakota eyeing each other, looking for an opening in the other's defense.

James tightened his grip on van Heerden's gun, his knuckles turning white under the strain. Van Heerden snarled in response, his eyes gleaming with a dangerous mix of fury and hatred, but his iron-like grip on the weapon didn't waver. Neither one was willing to surrender or lose ground in this deadly tug-of-war. James shifted his weight and attempted to twist the revolver from van Heerden's grasp. His muscles strained against the effort, every tendon in his arms screaming for relief.

A loud boom filled the room, the sound of a gunshot echoing off the walls, as van Heerden pulled the trigger. The bullet struck a nearby metal stool with force, ricocheting off it like a cracked bell ringing out an alarm. Hilda screamed and bolted out of the laboratory.

Dakota kicked, his outstretched foot contacting Bridgers' side. With fast reflexes fueled by the cocaine, Bridgers caught Dakota's leg. Pulling upwards with an unexpected strength, Bridgers forced Dakota to lose his balance, falling with a thud on the hard floor, surrounded by a sea of crushed cardboard boxes that did little to cushion his fall. The chemist was on top of Dakota before he recovered, his fingers curling around Dakota's throat in a vice-like grip.

With a ferocious growl, van Heerden shoved James into a nearby workbench, both their grips tightening on the gun as they engaged in a dangerous arm-wrestling match. The barrel of the revolver inched closer to James' face. His heart pounded in sync with each strained breath as he pushed back against van Heerden's relentless pressure.

James mustered every bit of strength in his body and twisted, wrenching van Heerden's wrist downwards towards the sharp edge of the workbench. Van Heerden yelped and relaxed his grip for a split second. James seized the opportunity to slam his adversary's wrist even harder onto the unforgiving surface.

The harsh echo of another gunshot resonated within the confined space. Any human cry of pain did not follow it. Instead, it was accompanied by an electric sizzle as the bullet found its mark on a nearby fuse box. A brilliant shower of sparks erupted from the damaged electrical system like an improvised fireworks display, then all the light disappeared abruptly.

James took a calculated risk and released his right hand's grip on the gun, opting to throw a punch in the direction where he hoped van Heerden's face would be. It was. His fist contacted van Heerden's jaw, the impact sending a satisfying shockwave up his arm. James launched another strike, this time aiming for van Heerden's gut. His knuckles connected, causing a grunt from his adversary.

Van Heerden staggered backward, his grasp on the revolver loosening just enough for James to wrench it free. But before he could transfer it to his right hand, a heavy microscope slammed into the side of his head with blinding force. Stars exploded in his vision, disorienting him and making him stumble to the left. Surprised, James tangled with a stool and crashed to the ground, the gun clattering from his grasp and skidding across the tiles.

James groped blindly for the weapon in the blackness. Van Heerden's feet thudded on the floor as he made his escape. James finally got hold of the gun and moved towards the sound of the door slamming shut. He tripped over another stool that he didn't even know was there. Unlike van Heerden, who knew this room intimately, James was at a disadvantage, not knowing its layout.

He fumbled around in the dark, attempting to reach the exit van Heerden and Hilda used. His hand found the doorknob at last, but it was locked. He pounded his fist on the door in frustration. Of course... just as he expected from someone trying to escape and stop anybody following him.

The only sound in the darkness came from the heavy panting and grunting of the two other men struggling. At last, everything quieted.

"And the winner is..." James called out, the gun at the ready.

Dakota's face appeared, illuminated by the flashlight he held. "Did you have any doubt?"

James grinned and lowered his weapon. "I would never bet against you."

"Bridgers was high," Dakota said, as he walked to James. "The drug gave him increased physical performance and confidence..." he glanced behind him and briefly flashed some light toward the form sprawled out on the floor "... for a while."

"He must have removed his work clothes before taking a hit to avoid cross-contamination," James said. He looked around the laboratory. "It'll take hours to search this place with a single flashlight. Let's get to our contact. The CIA can take over from here."

***

A taxi dropped the agents in front of a two-story house featuring a mixture of colonial and traditional Indian architecture. The grand, symmetrical facade was painted in earthy tones, and topped with a terra-cotta tile roof. Geometric designs adorned the exterior walls, and the arched window frames flanked the wooden shutters.

James and Dakota went up to the decorative wrought iron garden gate set in a stone wall ringing the property. James pressed the button on an intercom. A second later, a crisp voice crackled through the speaker.

"Yes?"

"Good evening, Mr. Sharma," James said. "Sorry to disturb you. We're looking for an address, but I can't read the writing well. It looks like 'Box 1142.'"

"Please come in." Mr. Sharma's accent spoke of somebody educated at an English university but with a clipped, almost mechanical, quality. "I will be happy to assist you."

With a click, a remote control unlocked the gate. Dakota swung it open, walking through with James close behind. As soon as they both entered the courtyard, the gate locked again. The pair shared a quick glance.

They stood in a well-maintained, serene garden of tropical plants and flowers. The home's second-story roofed the area, with the wall and wrought iron grilles sealing the space.

"No way out," Dakota said in a low tone. "And we're being covered. Inside right corner."

James casually turned, as though taking in the foliage, and spotted a gun barrel protruding from a slot in the house. "Uh-huh."

A central arched doorway opened and Mr. Sharma stepped out. He was an elegant, middle-aged Indian man with a mane of silver hair. He wore a cream-colored cotton dhoti, a long piece of cloth wrapped around his waist and legs. Completing the outfit was a white kurta, a knee-length tunic with straight cut, long sleeves, and a mandarin collar. He smiled.

"Welcome, gentleman," he said with a slight bow. "You're American, are you not? Where are you from?"

"Fort Hunt area," Dakota answered.

James dug into his pocket and pulled out a hollowed coin. Dakota did the same. "We hate to bother you, but could we have change? We may have to take another taxi."

"Certainly." Mr. Sharma took the coins from them. "It will take me a few moments. While you wait, why don't you admire that mural?" He gestured toward the art painted on one wall. He went back inside the house, closing the door. It locked.

James and Dakota wandered over to the colorful artwork depicting Radha and Krishna dancing. One eye of Krishna reflected the light — a lens.

"Smile for the birdie," James said.

After about five minutes, the front door opened again. Mr. Sharma strode over to James and Dakota. "Mr. Walker, Mr. Vagus, a pleasure to meet you both. I welcome you to India," he said, shaking their hands. He returned the hollowed coins which contained microfilmed copies of their credentials. "You are the first MIS-X agents I have encountered. Please, come in."

Mr. Sharma escorted them into the home's bright living room. The clean, white walls contrasted with the warmth and vibrancy of the red tile floor. Two cozy rattan couches, adorned with an array of colorful cushions, were positioned into an inviting "L" shape. A metal and rattan coffee table served as a centerpiece in front of them, a silver coffee set resting on it. Above one couch hung an intricate wooden carving. In each corner of the room, potted palms added a touch of greenery.

James and Dakota sat on one sofa while their host took the other one. He gestured toward the pot as an invitation, then he settled back and tented his fingers, ready to listen. The two teen agents poured themselves cups of coffee, then summed up their activities from Miami to arriving at Mr. Sharma's front door.

"I will send the local police to the George Town address," Mr. Sharma said as he stood. "At least they can secure the area." He left the room but returned only a few minutes later. He had a worried look on his face. "It seems there are already city officials present. The building at that location is on fire."

Chapter Thirteen

"Van Heerden's making tracks," Dakota said. "Just like in Miami."

James nodded. "I'll wager the fire department will discover the lab was ground zero for the inferno. Any evidence will be turned to ash." He locked onto Mr. Sharma's gaze. "Is there any way you could put a surveillance directive on the airports? Check the passenger lists for van Heerden and Hilda's names? Watch for them if they're using aliases? Stop them before they leave the country?"

Mr. Sharma folded his hands in front of him. His expression remained unreadable, yet not devoid of sympathy. "Mr. Vagus, I comprehend the gravity of what you both have told me. Please understand, a request like yours must flow through official inter-governmental channels, in this case between the United States and India. We would be looking at a process which involves embassies as well as intelligence agencies — like the CIA and the India Intelligence Bureau." He paused, allowing the weight of bureaucratic reality to sink in. "It may take days, even weeks, to obtain the clearance necessary for such an operation."

Dakota's jaw clenched, a visible sign of the frustration simmering within him. "So we just sit here while van Heerden beats feet? He could be anywhere in twenty-four hours."

James felt the same tightness gripping his chest, the helpless anger that clawed at him. His voice held steady despite the turmoil churning inside him. "We are on the brink of a possible worldwide food shortage, one that will cripple the West. This could lead to mass starvation."

"*Possible* food shortage. *Possible* starvation. But without concrete evidence concerning such an event, there is little I can do." A note of regret crept into Mr. Sharma's impassive tone. "Protocol is protocol, I'm afraid."

James and Dakota exchanged frustrated glances.

"We appreciate your candor," James said, keeping the sarcasm out of his tone. "Still, Mr. Sharma, there has to be something we can do now."

Mr. Sharma smiled, in a fatherly, but almost patronizing, way. "You two are new and young operatives. In the shadowy realm of counterintelligence, there are always rumors of numerous potential dangers, plots, and disasters circulating. Most of them are merely ploys to test, to probe, the opposing side's response. It is part of the game… a method to trace the paths on how intelligence is transmitted. This may be one of those situations. Nevertheless, I will prepare all the information required for your request. I will attempt to initiate it, but I cannot guarantee its success or even if it will be acted upon." Mr. Sharma sat back on the sofa, tented his fingers again, and closed his eyes. "For now, please describe the parties involved. Be thorough."

James and Dakota provided detailed descriptions of van Heerden and Hilda. When they were finished, Mr. Sharma opened his eyes and repeated the profiles back, each word a perfect echo of their own. After a moment, it was clear to James that the interview was at an end. He stood, followed by Dakota and Mr. Sharma.

"I appreciate your time, Mr. Sharma," James said. Dakota agreed with a nod.

"Of course. I'm sorry I can't be as much assistance as you desire," Mr. Sharma said. "Please, allow me to summon a taxi for you."

"Thank you," James said.

Mr. Sharma gave a slight bow. "By Sita and Rama, may everyone be blessed."

James and Dakota thanked Mr. Sharma again, then left, the wrought-iron gate locking behind them when they stepped onto the sidewalk. The noise of the city was a distant buzz underlining their thoughts of failure.

"Protocol," Dakota fumed. "Smith's going to love this."

"Except he'd most likely agree." James fished out his wallet. "Let's see if I have enough cash for cab fare." His fingers brushed over the crinkled edges of currency when a small piece of paper caught his attention — the pawn ticket from Miami. "Huh."

"What?" Dakota peered at what was in James' hand.

"We may not be at a dead end," James drawled.

"What are you holding?"

"I found this when I searched van Heerden's bungalow. It's a pawn ticket for a pocket watch." He held the paper up so Dakota could see it. "I told you van Heerden pulled out of there fast. This was jammed behind a drawer in his desk. You know, that sometimes happens when it's full. Either he forgot about it, or thought he took it when he was dumping the contents into a suitcase." James shrugged. "I thought it was funny. Van Heerden needed money so much he pawned his watch, but..." His voice trailed off as he thought.

"But..." Dakota prompted after a few silent seconds.

James held up one hand to quiet Dakota. A hunch curled in his head, its tendrils spreading through his brain like wildfire. "What if van Heerden needs to retrieve this?" he said, turning the ticket over in his hand.

Dakota raised an eyebrow. "What for? Van Heerden doesn't seem like a man who is moved by sentiment."

"I agree. However, he still may need the watch, not for sentimental reasons, but for information. It could hold important data or instructions that are too risky to trust with just anyone's memory, including his own. It's possible that the details are engraved on the case or hidden inside somewhere." James' thoughts were racing as he carefully arranged all the pieces in his mind. "He probably used a pawn shop as a sort of safe for the watch. It would have been easier than renting a bank safe deposit box and there would be less paperwork and fewer questions involved. And if he came under police investigation, they may not think to check a place like that. At least, not at first." He held up the piece of paper. "They might overlook something like this."

"Sure, but he must realize it's missing by now," Dakota pointed out, leaning against the gatepost, arms crossed.

"True, which means he can't just walk in and claim it — he must show this." James waved the paper.

"Would that stop him? Couldn't he use a duplicate? Redeem the loan anyway? Just pay it off?" Dakota asked.

"I'll bet that would be difficult without the correct identification. Cops keep a constant eye on pawn brokers, so records are required," James answered. "Not having a ticket would kick off a lengthy process. It could involve an affidavit or sworn statements. There even may be a waiting period."

"What can van Heerden do?"

"That leaves only one option," James concluded with a grim smile. "Breaking and entering."

A taxi trundled up. The pair climbed into the back seat.

"Let's get moving," Dakota said.

"Do you have your passport with you?" James said, determination setting into his voice.

Dakota nodded.

"Then we're traveling light. Aunt Martha can arrange for our luggage to be sent on." James turned to the driver. "Airport, please."

***

The neon sign of Fast Deal Pawn flickered, creating a sallow light on the empty street from the corner store. James and Dakota, exhausted after a cobbled-together series of flights from Madras to Miami, approached the building that was as tired as they were. James peered at the objects crowding the front window.

The dirty glass displayed an array of items: a gleaming French horn, a worn but well-loved guitar, delicate vases adorned with intricate patterns, antique lamps casting a warm glow, and a collection of clocks ticking away in unison. The shop interior was as dark as the surrounding night, with only the suggestion of more overflowing shelves and showcases. With a terse nod to Dakota, he led the way to the side entrance, his hand reaching for the doorknob. Locked.

"You didn't expect it to be open, did you?" Dakota's eyes scanned the shadows.

"Hope springs eternal," James sighed, a wry smile fleeting across his face. "Maybe the pawnbroker was working late."

The shuffle of boots on the pavement and a loud belch broke their moment of silent communication. A figure emerged from the alley and staggered toward them. The man's clothes hung off him in tattered layers, and his gait was unsteady, the stench of alcohol preceding him.

"Ya missed 'im," the bum slurred, pointing a grimy finger at the shop door.

"Oh? Who did we miss?" Dakota asked with a friendly smile. "The pawnbroker?"

"Nah, not him. The other fella, the one that came by 'bout..." The drunk held up his bottle and sloshed the remaining third of booze in it, "... half a bottle ago." He wheezed a laugh.

Dakota joined in with an appreciative chuckle. "What did he look like, this other guy?"

"Oh, a real gentleman type, ya know? Dressed in real fancy threads." The man took a swig. He wiped his mouth with the back of one dirty hand. "Not from around here."

"Go on," Dakota prodded gently. "If it wasn't the pawnbroker, who was it?"

"I dunno, I told you that," the bum said with irritation. "Used a key, opened the door smooth-like. In and out, ten minutes tops." He hiccuped, then grinned toothlessly. "Saw his car make a U-turn, went back the way it came. Back to the land of soft beds and fine liquor." He hoisted the bottle in a toast.

"Thank you," Dakota said, pressing some bills into the man's hand. The money disappeared into the folds of the drunk's coat as quickly as it had appeared. Dakota took hold of the bum's shoulders and stared deeply into his eyes. He spoke simply and kindly, but with an intensity James hadn't heard before, as though Dakota was summoning emotion from the past. "Sober up, man. Take that monkey off your back."

The bum pulled back from Dakota, a peaceful looking crossing his face for a moment. "Yeah, I will." He wandered off.

"Looks like we just missed our quarry," Dakota said to James.

"Timing is everything." There was a sharp edge of frustration in James' voice. He peered into the pawnshop again.

Dakota said, "We have company," as the sound of a motor pulling up to the curb and crackling radio transmissions filled the night air. A pulsing red light slashed the night.

James turned to face the two police officers as they stepped out of their patrol car.

"You guys looking for something?" asked the first police officer.

"An item that was pawned in here," James said.

"And I guess you want it back?" challenged the second cop.

"Yes, that's the general idea." Keeping his right hand visible, James reached into his hip pocket for his wallet. He handed over his driver's license and a federal government ID — only labeling him as an employee in the "Intelligence Services". Dakota followed suit, presenting his own similar forms of identification.

The first officer accepted the IDs and scanned through them. As his eyes flicked back and forth between James, Dakota, and the identity cards, a brief look of suspicion crossed his face. "I need to run a check on these."

James shrugged. "Of course."

The policeman walked back to his patrol car and sat down in the passenger seat. He spoke into his radio, a muffled conversation that ended with a clear "what? You're kiddin'" from him. He came back to James and Dakota.

"Credentials check out. They're legit," the cop said to his partner in a surprised tone, handing the identification and licenses back. "Sorry for having to do that, but you guys look too young to be..."

"That's the point," Dakota said, as he slid the cards into his wallet.

"Yeah, I guess. "The policeman turned to the other cop. "We have orders to cooperate." He directed his attention back to James. "What exactly is your business here?"

"Let's just say we're trying to get our hands on something of great importance to national security." James reclaimed his IDs. He jerked his head towards the store. "Anyway, we can have the owner to let us in?"

Nodding, the second officer made his way back to his cruiser, radio crackling as he spoke into it. Time trickled by. James began to pace like a caged animal, while Dakota stood absolutely still. At last, headlights cut through the darkness, and a late-model Lincoln Continental pulled up to the curb. The streetlights twinkled off the spotless white paint like stars.

"He does well for himself," James said to Dakota. Dakota nodded.

A small man emerged from the car, looking disheveled and quite bald. It was clear that his sleep had been disrupted, and he was not happy about it. The pawnbroker grumbled about the early hour and how much he paid in taxes, stating he deserved a good night's rest after working hard all day.

"Mr. Highgate, these gentlemen work for the federal government." The first officer gestured toward James and Dakota. "They need to get into your shop. They say it is a matter of the greatest importance."

"We thought you wouldn't want us to break in," James added with the utmost politeness.

Highgate, unimpressed and unamused, glared at them, and mumbled to himself "What they think I have in here, an atom bomb?" He unlocked the door and waved everybody inside. "Here we are," Mr. Highgate said gruffly. "The normal open time is nine. In the AM."

With a harsh buzz, the fluorescent lights flickered to life overhead, casting the interior of the pawnshop in an unflattering glare. Instruments of every kind lined the walls, from dusty guitars to tarnished trumpets, creating a symphony of mismatched shapes and sizes.

Jewelry of all kinds sat in the cracked glass cases, their once-sparkling gems now dulled by years of neglect. Shelves of almost any other type of object, from vacuum cleaners to radios, filled the shop's cluttered interior.

James's gaze zeroed in on the counter. Two crisp twenty-dollar bills lay beside a folded sheet of paper.

"Somebody's been in here!" Mr. Highgate pushed Dakota to one side. "Outta my way, Tonto."

James cast a quick glance at Dakota. His partner's eyes hardened, but that was all the emotion he showed.

"Cheap alarm system!" Highgate ranted. "It should've gone off! I'm gonna give that company a piece of my mind!"

"Careful, Mr. Highgate. I don't think you have much to spare," James commented dryly. That warranted a slight smile from Dakota. James' fingers brushed aside the money, revealing the note beneath. The message was simple: "For the redemption of one silver hunter watch, $40." The signature at the bottom read "Van Heerden, M.D." He held up the twenties. "These are yours, I believe."

Highgate reached for them, but James yanked them back. "First, please check if a silver German hunter pocket watch is missing from your inventory."

Glowering at James, Highgate selected a key from a full ring and opened a metal lock box. He slid out a tray containing all types of watches. One slot was empty. Highgate tapped the vacant space. "It's gone. It should be right there."

James handed the money to the pawnbroker, who snatched it away like a toad catching a fly with its tongue. He walked away, grumbling. "Didn't even get my interest. Didn't even make a dime out of this whole transaction."

"Mr. Highgate, would you please check the store to see if anything else is missing?" the second policeman asked.

"Yeah, yeah. Sure." Mr. Highgate moved away, pocketing the cash and muttering to himself.

"So our drinking buddy outside saw van Heerden entering the shop," James said. "He must have had a duplicate key."

"You know who got in here? And how?" the first cop said. "Give us the information, and we'll put out an APB on him."

James shook his head. "We need him free... to lead us to his headquarters."

Both the officers nodded.

Dakota leaned closer, looking at the note. "So you were right about van Heerden needing the watch. He discovered he didn't have the pawn ticket, so he let himself in to retrieve it. What do you make of that?"

James tapped his fingers on the counter. "Van Heerden is very organized. He has to be to run an operation that has taken place in different parts of the world... obtain chemicals... find chemists to work on his project."

"And move the whole thing on a moment's notice when it's uncovered by a couple of nosy young guys," Dakota put in with a grin.

James grinned back and nodded. "You bet. I wouldn't be surprised if, when he pawned the watch, he thought ahead of a possible situation like this. He got his hands on a spare key through various means. He could have swiped it, created a plasticine mold of it to have a copy made, or found some other way to make a duplicate. Just in case."

"So he had all of this planned?" Dakota asked.

"As a backup. One he didn't expect to use." James tapped the paper.

"He brought the note with him, all prepared?" Dakota pointed to it.

James shook his head. "He didn't plan that, though."

One cop took a step forward to look closer at the paper. "Why do you say that?"

"It's too casual," James explained. "He wrote this in a hurry. It's on a torn half-sheet of paper, which he probably had in his pocket. And he most likely used that pen." James tilted his head toward a lone ballpoint lying on the counter. "It's the only one nearby. The others are stored in that mug by the register. This 'receipt' was an act of pure bravado." He flipped over the paper, revealing part of an invoice printed on the other side.

"One barrel of 2,4-Dichlorophenoxyacetic acid," Dakota read. "That must be one of the ingredients he uses."

James nodded. "Either through carelessness or arrogance, van Heerden has given us a lead."

"Then let's follow it," Dakota said, his voice low and steady. After a second, he put his hand on James' arm. "Or he's planned this, too. Planted a clue. Following it could send us on a wild goose chase... or into a trap."

"That's possible. Van Heerden is intelligent." James turned to Mr. Highgate, whose irritation had been steadily mounting. "We'll need a phone book if you don't mind. The Yellow Pages."

With a grunt of disapproval, the pawnbroker shuffled to a cluttered desk, retrieved the thick directory of ads, and slapped it onto the counter. James flipped through the categories until he found what he was looking for. With a decisive rip, he tore out the page for "Industrial Equipment & Supplies" and folded it neatly, tucking it away like a prized possession.

"Hey! You can't just — " Mr. Highgate began, but Dakota cut him off with a fierce gaze.

"The telephone company will give you another copy. For free," Dakota stated flatly.

James faced the policemen. "Thank you for your cooperation, officers. Please do not mention us in your night's report. This was a simple response to a false burglar alarm."

The two cops nodded.

"And Mr. Highgate, the same for you," James went on. "Take the pocket watch off your records in the normal way of being redeemed. We were not here. If any word of our presence in your establishment this evening leaks out... well, keep in mind, we have contacts with the Internal Revenue Service."

Mr. Highgate gulped, then bobbed his head up and down nervously. "Just a false burglar alarm. Cheap alarm system."

"Thank you for your cooperation," Dakota nailed the pawnbroker with a dark glare. He raised one hand, palm out. "How, paleface."

"Let's get going," James said, heading towards the door, Dakota falling into step beside him. They moved as one entity, an unbreakable alliance, as they stepped outside into the night.

They stopped on the sidewalk and Dakota spat out a Cherokee word under his breath. James looked at him. "I don't know that word. What does it mean?"

Dakota grinned. "I won't tell you, James, because you are not one."

"I'm glad I'm not. It didn't sound friendly."

"It isn't."

James chuckled as he pulled out the page he tore from the phone book. "Let's check those companies first thing in the morning."

"Agreed," Dakota replied. "We'll see if that is their invoice, and did any of them sell that stuff to van Heerden. And when. If it was part of a large, recent order, maybe we could see a delivery address."

"With any luck," James yawned. "What time is it?"

Dakota checked his watch. "Late. Very late."

"Let's find a hotel. Then we'll call Aunt Martha from there to arrange a rental car and forward our luggage." James gestured down the block. "There's a major street. We should be able to pick up a taxi there."

Chapter Fourteen

T HE DULL ROUTINE OF visiting the industrial equipment and supply companies paid off. James and Dakota discovered the source of the invoice and the delivery address: an island in the Florida Keys. After making plans and requisitioning supplies, the two now stood on the deck of their borrowed vessel, the gentle sound of waves lapping against the hull filling the quiet night air.

The inky blackness of the sea melted into the night sky. Off to the port, Skeleton Cay appeared as a small blip of land surrounded by endless darkness. The faint silhouettes of trees stood against the star-studded canvas above, giving the five-acre island an eerie and mysterious presence.

"After what happened with the Usurper, I still can't believe the CIA trusted you with another boat," James said as he leaned overboard, placing a bundle in the ocean. He yanked a ripcord and a two-man raft unfurled, inflating with a pop and a loud hiss. He lashed the cord from it to a cleat, then joined Dakota.

"I had to put down a huge deposit," Dakota said, pulling out a haversack.

James laughed as they packed the equipment they thought they would need: incendiaries compact enough to fit in a pocket, a tranquilizer-laden dart gun, an electronic stethoscope, as well as the motel kit, lock pick knives, and a miniature camera.

"Let's hope that address van Heerden gave on the invoice was accurate," James said, glancing at the shadowed island, "and we're not about to interrupt some rich guy's idyllic Florida vacation."

"Or this whole thing is a waste of time, or we're about to walk into a trap," Dakota said, slinging the haversack over one shoulder.

"That's what I like about you," James said. "You always see the bright side of things."

Dakota grinned. "Just my lovable nature, I guess."

James let out a groan while tugging on a snug black knit cap, concealing his blonde locks. Dakota was already wearing a similar outfit, his long hair tucked away under his own watch cap. Both were clad in head-to-toe black: turtleneck sweaters, pants, and sturdy boots. With the agility of predators, they boarded the raft, leaving barely a ripple in their wake.

James took a moment to take in their surroundings, catching sight of the shadowy outline of the island looming on the horizon. "Are you nervous?"

"You better believe it," Dakota replied.

"Dakota, has it hit you yet? What we're doing on this mission? Not just what we're about to do, but the whole thing? Who we are? What we are?" James shook his head as though disbelieving the reality. "It's not exactly what I had in mind after graduation."

"Me neither. But way down, man... but, I don't know, doubt and fear are creeping in," Dakota went on. "Can we prove ourselves and accomplish this? Are we up to it? If we fail... "

"You know Dakota, I was speaking with a wise person, sitting under a palm tree on the beach the other day," James said. "We were talking about learning to swim... being thrown in the deep end. And as we looked over the ocean, he told me that he didn't intend to drown."

Dakota locked eyes with James and gave a half-smile. "Neither do I."

"And with the two of us on the case, failure is not an option," James stated. He paused for a second. "You know, before now, the most exciting thing I've done in my life was hiding Sister Helen's dentures." He shrugged and flashed an embarrassed smile. "I almost feel guilty admitting this, but I'm enjoying myself."

"Me too, brother, me too," Dakota grinned.

"Ready?" James asked though it was more an affirmation than a question.

"Always," Dakota answered, his voice low but firm. "It's a five-mile row."

"We both need the workout," James said. He untied the cord.

With a push, they set themselves adrift towards Skeleton Cay. James gripped the oars with determination, his muscles flexing under the strain as they cut through the dark waters. Dakota matched his rhythm, their synchronized efforts propelling their small vessel forward with stealthy urgency. The sturdy fabric of the raft whispered against the calm sea as they paddled. The two rowed in silence.

As they approached the shore after ninety minutes, James' stomach clenched with a mix of excitement and nerves. Even though he never played organized sports in school, it was how he imagined a football team must feel before a big game. He sensed Dakota was the same way as they neared their destination.

The Cay loomed closer. They could now make out the outlines of mahogany and palm trees towering over the shoreline, whispering in the sea breeze. They reached the shore, stowing their oars and climbing onto the beach, their boots sinking slightly into the wet sand.

They concealed the raft beneath a tangle of roots and a camouflage of fallen leaves. Pulling out their flashlights, covered with red lenses, they made sure no trace of their landing was visible. They kept the beams pointed at the ground and headed into the forest, Dakota taking the lead. The two moved inland, the jungle swallowing them whole.

"Listen to that," James said, a note of awe in his voice.

The place was alive with nocturnal symphonies—the croaking of frogs, the chirping of crickets, and the occasional splash of fish leaping in the shallows. The trees stood like sentinels over the island. In the distance, some animals rustled through the underbrush, while overhead, the silhouette of a diving seabird cut across the star-studded sky. He took a moment to appreciate the vibrant life around them—even in the dark. James was so entranced by the sights and sounds he bumped into Dakota.

"Watch where you're going, you tourist!" Dakota hissed.

"Sorry," James whispered back.

"The dock is on the south shore, so the main house must be close to it," Dakota said in a low voice. James nodded.

The two agents melded into the shadows, the darkness their ally as they made their way toward the unknown on Skeleton Cay. They advanced with silent steps, flickering through the island's dense greenery until a sudden rustling halted them. Voices sliced through the night air. James and Dakota doused their flashlights and ducked behind some bushes.

Two men, their outlines etched against the darker backdrop, walked by while talking. They each casually held a rifle in their hands. James and Dakota watched them as they disappeared into the jungle, their boots crunching on the underbrush.

James cocked his head, listening to the language. "That's not German. The intonation pattern is different. Maybe Czech... or Polish."

"Did you see their posture?" Dakota whispered, his voice barely more than a breath. "Military training. And I'll bet they're carrying infantry-issue rifles."

"Van Heerden's foreign reinforcements, courtesy of his new governmental sponsor," James concluded. "This island is isolated enough to permit clandestine water landings, like we did."

"Well, if those two are going that way, let's find out where they came from," Dakota said. After James nodded in agreement, they moved down a trail.

They soon came across a stone outbuilding. The only sign of life was a lone guard perched on a crate illuminated by a single barn light above the door. His eyes were fixated on the ground, and he flicked away an ash from his cigarette with a bored expression.

James nudged Dakota and pointed to the side of the man's seat. Stenciled on the wooden slats was the name of the Miami supply firm.

Dakota smoothly removed the haversack from his back and retrieved a small gun. A bit larger than a fountain pen but resembling one, it used a powerful spring to fire a single small dart, so sharp and tiny it could be mistaken for an insect's sting when it struck. And once the projectile entered the human body, it dissolved without a trace.

Signaling with a tilt of his head, Dakota's form merged into the night as he stalked his target. James knew the dart gun was a mere extension of Dakota's concentration and will, poised and ready. The guard remained oblivious, the dictionary definition of a sitting duck.

James positioned himself at an angle where he could keep watch on the surroundings. After a few minutes, Dakota peered from behind a palm tree. He brought the gun to his right eye and held it there. He steadied his aim by pressing his wrist against the trunk. A pause as Dakota locked onto his target, then he twisted the pen's front ring a half-turn. The dart gun emitted a hushed puff of air as it fired.

The projectile found its mark. The guard's curse was muffled as he slapped at the back of his neck, confused and disoriented. He looked around, swatting around himself as though trying to wave off an annoying insect.

James waited as minutes ticked by. The tranquilizer slowly began to take effect, causing the consciousness of the guard to crumble like a sandcastle against the relentless ocean. His head drooped forward and then jerked back upright before lolling down again. He became more limp, his shoulders slumping, followed by the rest of his body, so he resembled a rag doll on a shelf. Then, with little fanfare, he swayed slightly from side to side, then toppled off the crate to the dirt.

"Smooth," James said as he stepped out from his cover as Dakota joined him. With the guard out of the way, James and Dakota slipped through the outbuilding's entrance. They flicked on their flashlights, playing the beams over rows of shelves laden with chemicals. A sharp, tangy scent floated in the air.

On a small table, there were a couple of smaller boxes that resembled the ones from the Madras factory. James reached for one and opened it up, revealing several vials of the Golden Blight. The dangerous granules inside appeared to glow in the beam of his flashlight. He passed the box to Dakota.

"Here's a gift for Smith," James said in a low voice.

Dakota pretended to read something written on the cardboard. "To Smith, with love. From James," Dakota cooed. "Aw, how sweet."

James shot Dakota an exasperated look. Slipping the package into the haversack, Dakota pulled out the two incendiary devices and handed one to James. The three-inch by five-inch cases, filled with a jelled petroleum fuel, created a long-lasting flame when ignited.

"What delay?" Dakota asked.

"Set it for... " James checked his watch. "Three hours. That should give us enough time to poke around and clear out before the show starts."

Dakota nodded. They located a green-painted mark and removed the guards protecting fragile copper tubes. With a strong grip, they crushed the tubes until the glass vials inside shattered. The action released a corrosive liquid that ate away at a restraining wire. When that broke, it freed a striker to spark the match head to ignite a fire.

James took the safety strips off the case and scanned the room. He grinned when his eyes landed on a box with a clear warning label that read "Flammable." He gestured to Dakota, who looked over and smiled, giving a thumbs up. James put his incendiary in behind the crate while Dakota placed the other behind a nearby one. As they straightened up, the bombastic, dramatic music of the "Ride of the Valkyries" shattered the quiet night.

"Wagner. Figures," James said to himself.

Cracking open the door, James peeked out at the guard. He still lay on the dirt. The two agents slipped out of the outbuilding, softly closing the door behind them.

"At least that racket gives us a direction to the main house," Dakota said. He started to slip through the dense vegetation with such speed and ease that James had to ask him quietly, "Slow down!" so he could keep up with his partner.

The mansion loomed ahead, its Mediterranean architecture a cross between elegant Spanish styling and a fortress. They approached with caution. Only a single lit window broke the mansion's dark facade, the Valkyries singing "Hojotoho! Hojotoho! Heiaha! Heiaha!" bursting out.

James and Dakota circled past the window to a shadowed French door. James sprinted to it and tested the handle. It opened, and he peeked inside.

It was at one time a library. Rich, mahogany built-in shelves lined the walls, matching the gleaming wood floor. A wrought iron chandelier hung from the exposed beams crossing the ceiling. The space was bare, devoid of any furniture or books. The bookshelves were broken on the opposite side by sturdy doors with brass handles, their surfaces polished to a shine. James beckoned to Dakota, who joined him.

The opera music seemed to come from behind one of the doors, echoing as if coming down a long hall. Dakota padded to the other door like a cat and pressed his ear against the dark wood. After a few moments, he shook his head. Without hesitation, he inched open the door and stepped into the next room, with James directly following him. The room was shrouded in darkness. Dakota flicked on his flashlight, as did James.

They stood in an area smaller than the library and now appeared to function as an office. Along one wall stood a table with a chair, with a shortwave set placed on top of it. A basic desk and chair were situated across from the radio. There were no other furnishings or decorations, allowing the dull metal of a wall safe to reflect in their flashlight beams.

The music stopped. Silence filled the mansion.

James walked to the safe, holding out one hand in a silent command. Dakota handed him the electronic stethoscope. James attached the microphone next to the dial and slipped on the stethoscopic earphones. He plugged both into the amplifier and took a deep breath before slowly turning the knob.

The metallic clicking sound of the tumblers filled his ears until he heard a slight "drop" sound — he had found one correct position in the combination. Moistening his lips with his tongue and holding his body tense, he closed his eyes and concentrated, beads of sweat forming on his forehead as he uncovered the remaining numbers of the combination, one methodical dial twist at a time. At last, a low thud came through the earphones. It was the welcome sound of the lock unlatching.

With a grin flashing across his face, he returned the electronic stethoscope to Dakota and swung open the metal door. File folders lay inside. On top of them was a small black book. James picked it up and flipped through the pages as Dakota held a flashlight on it.

The book contained a list of names and addresses belonging to people located in the main wheat-producing regions of the Western World, such as Kansas, Punjab in India, and New South Wales in Australia. Each entry had a note indicating the "Versanddatum" — "shipping date" in German — along with a specific month and day.

James realized he had in his hands van Heerden's network of contacts. These were the agents who would carry out the plan to spread the Golden Blight throughout the fields, triggering widespread devastation to crops.

James passed the book to Dakota, who secreted it away into his haversack, and then James pulled out a folder and placed it open on the desk. He pantomimed taking a picture to ask for the miniature camera.

Dakota's hand shot out, gripping James' arm. There was no need for words. James knew that his partner had picked up on something. Replacing the file, James closed and locked the safe. The two glided out of the mansion through the library's French doors. They retreated into the shadows just as light flooded the office they'd left. James let out a relieved breath as they crouched among the foliage.

"Stůj! Ruce vzhůru!" The harsh command shattered the silence. James and Dakota spun around to see the barrel of a rifle pointed at them, held by a scowling guard.

"Czech," James said as he and Dakota stood, raising their hands.

The guard's gun waved them back inside. They complied, stepping back into the lion's den. Van Heerden and Hilda waited, an unhappy reception committee. When the doctor saw James and Dakota, his sigh was a study of disgruntlement. His gaze flickered over them like a host worn out by unwelcome holiday guests. "You two again," he muttered under his breath.

James switched to Cherokee to bark an order. "Get the book out of here."

With a distracting shout, James lunged at the guard, his muscles electrified. The scuffle between the two broke the stillness of the mansion as they engaged in a fierce struggle over control of the rifle.

Dakota burst out the French doors, his heart pounding as he raced into the embrace of the night. From inside the house, the sharp blast of a rifle echoed through the air, followed by two more shots in rapid succession. Aimed at him or James?

The piercing clanging of an alarm bell shattered the quiet of the darkness. Dakota's boots skidded on the underbrush, his breath a measured cadence. Bobbing, weaving, jumping, dodging, ducking... his instincts took over as he efficiently threaded his way through the foliage. He became the ghost of his past, the one he seldom allowed himself to recall — those days of running, hiding, surviving. Outwitting his searchers.

A clearing loomed ahead. Dakota and a guard entered it at the same time, startling each other. He dropped the haversack, muscles tensing. The guard, equally surprised by Dakota's sudden appearance, fumbled with his rifle. Dakota charged at the guard, using his momentum to throw off the man's balance.

The guard stumbled backward but regained his footing and swung his rifle around like a club. Dakota ducked under the wild swing and retaliated with a swift punch to the man's midsection. As Dakota landed the punch, he felt a sharp pain shooting through his knuckles — this guy was solid! He winced but didn't let it slow him down.

The man staggered slightly back from the blow. He swung his rifle at Dakota once again. But Dakota dodged the weapon a second time. He scooped up handfuls of sandy soil and flung it into the guard's eyes.

Blinded and disoriented, the guard stumbled backward. With a fierce grunt, Dakota ripped the rifle from the guard's grasp and hurled it deep into the dense foliage, where it would be nearly impossible to retrieve.

The fight raged on, a primal battle between two beasts, each relying on their raw strength to overpower the other. They grappled and traded blows, both trying to gain the upper hand.

Pretending to lose ground, Dakota allowed himself to be backed towards a fallen log. The guard saw an opportunity and charged. But in a split second, Dakota stepped to the side, grabbed the guard's shoulder, and used his momentum to send him flying over the log.

Twisting in midair, the guard landed hard on his back. Straddling the man, Dakota delivered a series of punches that ended the struggle. He collapsed beside his unconscious opponent — exhausted but victorious.

Panting, Dakota climbed to his feet and snatched up the haversack. Through the trees, he heard the welcoming sound of the ocean. He staggered through the forest to the beach and uncovered the raft. He pushed it into the water and climbed in. He paused, looking back at the island.

Dakota couldn't shake James from his mind. They had formed a close bond during training. They had been an unstoppable duo on this mission, closely working with each other every step of the way. James was someone he liked and who also liked him... showing it was okay to care for people, to let them into his world. So how could he abandon his friend... for that is what Dakota considered him now... to an unthinkable fate?

James had saved him from van Heerden's torture... and that was certainly in James' future if he was still alive. It was only right for Dakota to return the favor. He should go back. He had to go back. All the fibers of his soul screamed for him to do that.

But they were on a crucial mission, with secrets and information that were bigger than their personal ties... or even their lives. The book he carried contained critical data about a threat to the Western world's food supply, and he was the only one who could see this through to the end.

"A na da yo ha, James. I am with you. Forgive me," Dakota said, voice barely stirring the night air. Settling at the oars, his strokes cut through the water as he headed back to the boat.

Chapter Fifteen

J AMES' HANDS SNAPPED OUT, seizing the guard's rifle with a desperate grip. Skin slid on steel as they wrestled for control of the weapon. Dakota, swift as a shadow, darted through the French doors into the night.

The guard retaliated with a fast knee to James' midsection. Doubling over in pain, James gasped for breath but refused to let go. The loud ringing of an alarm bell played discordant background music to the battle in the library.

A shot exploded, earsplitting in the confined space, and a plume of plaster dust ballooned from the wall where the bullet found its mark. The struggle escalated, their dance deadly and erratic, sending two more bullets careening into the ceiling. Chunks of rubble rained down like the aftermath of a storm.

The guard's snarl reverberated as he shoved James away and wrenched the rifle free from his grasp. James hurtled backward, his body slamming into the barren bookshelves with a deafening crash. The guard's eyes glinted with malice, the barrel now a rigid line of certainty aimed at James. Just then, the alarm was abruptly cut, plunging the room into a sinister silence. Van Heerden moved away from the button placed on the wall.

"Your persistence," Van Heerden began, strolling forward with the nonchalance of a man observing insects in a jar, "is nothing short of irritating."

James glowered, chest heaving, every sinew alert and waiting. Van Heerden paused, his gaze flickering toward the open doors where Dakota had vanished.

"The other one was caught in the Miami warehouse, wasn't he?" van Heerden asked.

"Perhaps he is also a wealthy orphan," Hilda said dryly.

"No doubt. And now here you two are, working in tandem. How interesting." Van Heerden's words were edged with accusation, each one hanging in the air like a judge ready to pronounce the death sentence. "Tell me, are you and the other one operating alone as a team, or do you have even more confederates waiting?"

James locked eyes with van Heerden, his expression unyielding and filled with icy determination. Van Heerden gave a small nod, and the guard slammed the butt of his rifle onto James' stomach. Agony exploded through his abdomen, leaving him gasping for breath as he crumpled to his knees. The force of the blow sent his vision spinning and the taste of blood flooded his mouth, but he fought against the urge to vomit and remained resolute in the face of their brutality.

"Mr. Vagus, can you hear me?" Van Heerden's voice, clinical and detached, sliced through the haze of pain. James nodded. "Your friend is likely scurrying for assistance. But he needs to escape this island first. Alive. An unlikely occurrence. Stand with your hands clasped behind your head."

With effort, James forced himself upright and did as he was told. The guard watched with a predatory, amused sneer.

"It is time for final preparations. This incident shouldn't upset things too much," van Heerden said to Hilda. He gave an order to the guard in German, "If he moves, shoot him." He turned to James. "I just told — "

"I know what you said," James replied. "I speak German fluently."

"My, my. You are full of surprises, Mr. Vagus," van Heerden said. He and Hilda went into the office.

James steadied his breathing and listened. He couldn't see them, but the walls did little to muffle their conversation — their voices weaving through the heavy air and into James' awareness.

"A hidden compartment in the pocket watch, really?" Hilda's tone held a mixture of surprise and admiration. "And what is in there?"

"A small piece of paper with three words written on it. Three little code words to control the final fate of my project." Van Heerden's voice was smug, self-satisfied, assured. "One starts it, one holds it at bay, and one ends it with destruction of all evidence. At midnight, my agents will hear my short-wave transmission of one of those."

"Which one of them will be transmitted tonight?" she teased, laughter echoing into the empty library.

"I'm certain you are able to guess." Van Heerden's chuckle was low and conspiratorial. The sound of clicking switches filtered to James.

"What if you don't give any command?" Hilda asked.

"My agents are not ideological. Without my tight control, they would use the contents of the vials for their own goals in their own time. Whatever would give them the most money, probably. For my plan to work, the strike must be coordinated and worldwide. Surprise and speed are of the essence." Van Heerden was quiet for a moment. "There. The radio is set at the correct wavelength. Now to attend to our unwelcome visitor."

James' mind raced, even as his body remained motionless under the vigilant guard's watch. Code words

— midnight broadcast — the pieces clicked together, forming a picture more chilling than the steel muzzle pointed at his chest. It was clear that van Heerden was ready to trigger the distribution of the Golden Blight... tonight.

A disruption shattered the library's stale tension, as another man rushed through the French doors with a question sharp and urgent. "Kde je van Heerden?"

James' captor hardly shifted, a mere tilt of the head directing the newcomer toward the office. The second guard jogged into the other room.

"Der Andere ist weg. Wir können ihn auf der Insel nicht finden," the words tumbled from the second guard in German so bad it was obviously not the man's native language. But the message, clear and unmistakable, sent a current of hope surging through James' veins.

Dakota had evaded capture. He'd gotten off the island, the precious book of contacts in hand. James knew nothing would stop his partner from finishing the mission now. No matter what happened to James now, he knew he had won.

Van Heerden's curse was a snarl that carried from the next room to the library, heavy with frustration. "Nevertheless, time is still our ally," van Heerden said. "An hour, maybe more, before help arrives — if they make it at all. Hilda, ready the boat. Be prepared for an immediate departure when I board."

Heels clicking on the wood floors, Hilda left the office, strode past James without so much as a glance, and out the other door. Van Heerden entered and walked up to James.

Van Heerden's voice took on a forced, apologetic tone that belied the cruelty in his eyes. "I have many questions for you, Mr. Vagus, so many questions. But first an apology. We are pressed for time, and I must expedite our... conversation. I'm afraid we will dispense with the niceties and move immediately to the main event. We may even have time for something enjoyable... for me."

"More medical experimentation?" James snarled.

Van Heerden smiled. "Oh, no. Far, far worse." He faced the guard. "Vorbereiten Sie ihn zum Verhör." He turned back to James, his smile a glacial crack in his composed facade. "I'm sure you don't need a translation for that."

A chill ran down James' spine as the guard's grin broadened — a lion's smirk before the pounce. Every muscle in James' body tensed. "No, I don't. You said 'Prepare him for interrogation.'"

***

Dakota's fingers curled tightly around the radio microphone, his knuckles whitening as Smith's voice crackled through the static.

"You have in your possession the contact list and a sample of the Golden Blight," Smith said with bureaucratic detachment after Dakota completed his report.

"Yes, sir," Dakota responded, fingering the small book in his other hand.

"And you said Mr. Vagus...?" Smith prodded, the question a sharp edge in the night air.

"He didn't make it off the island," Dakota's response was terse.

"Do you know if he is still alive?" Smith pressed.

"I don't know. I heard three gunshots," was all Dakota could offer, the uncertainty gnawing at him. "But if he is alive, van Heerden won't let him wish for anything but death."

"You both received interrogation resistance training —"

"A simulation isn't reality, Smith!" Dakota cut in.

There was a pause. "It is most unfortunate about Mr. Vagus. He had promise," came Smith's cool response.

"Maybe you should've told him that during training instead of pushing him so hard," Dakota snapped.

"Mr. Walker, this isn't about my management style!" Smith fired back. "Standby." The radio went silent for a moment. "Here is some good news. There is a group of SEALs at the Naval Air Station Key West for some additional instruction and are now en route to your location. They'll secure the location. ETA in approximately one hour."

"That gives me time to extricate James," Dakota said.

"Negative. You may jeopardize the mission," Smith said. "Your presence might tip off van Heerden that something's up."

"I'm going back for James," Dakota stressed.

"Mr. Walker, I expressly forbid you to return to the island," Smith said, his voice strong. Dakota could almost see Smith's face turning red.

"Mr. Smith, I expressly disobey your order! Out." Dakota shouted into the mike and hammered his fist on the radio set's power switch.

The boat bobbed softly on the stillness of the water as Dakota pulled up the anchor. He steered the vessel carefully towards the shore, hoping that the darkness and lack of running lights would hide his approach. Once again, he dropped anchor before boarding the raft to make his way to the island. The small vessel would be faster than swimming and he knew he'd need it to bring back James — alive or dead. He secured his dagger in his belt and jumped into the raft, paddling steadily towards the shore with precise strokes.

He landed on the beach and quickly hid the raft behind some large rocks. Ahead of him, the dense tropical vegetation loomed a dark and potentially dangerous barrier. He made his way inland with caution, every sense on high alert for signs of danger.

Dakota crouched in back of a massive tree at the sound of heavy military boots crunching through the foliage. He waited until a man, dressed in olive green, came around a bend. In one swift and silent movement, Dakota lunged at him, hammering the edge of his hand down sharply on the guard's neck. The guard fell unconscious to the ground. Dakota rolled the body so it was concealed by a thick blanket of ferns.

He continued up the trail. The house came into view, the library, and office lights shining like beacons. Then it came — a scream, raw, guttural, full of pain — tearing the veil of night.

James.

Dakota grimaced, and his gut clenched at the sound. Two more cries came in quick succession, then stopped, leaving a silence that was somehow more terrifying. He pushed his way through the undergrowth until he was outside the house. He peered through the French door into the library.

Inside, with his wrists bound tightly above his head, James dangled limp from a thick rope attached to the wooden beam. He was stripped to the waist. His torso, crisscrossed with welts and burns, glistened with sweat mixed in with some blood. The guard stood behind him, gripping one of James' bare feet as if shoeing a horse, snapping a leather strap across the naked sole. James' head lolled on his chest.

"Halt!" van Heerden said to the guard, then walked over to James. He took hold of the cross around James' neck and smirked. "Wasn't much help, was it?"

His hand shot out, yanking James' head back by a fistful of blond hair. With clinical indifference, he pried open an eyelid, examining the unfocused blue eye beneath. He dropped James' head and moved to a medical bag perched on a shelf. His fingers were deft as they prepared a hypodermic needle, the sharp glint of metal catching the light as he injected its contents into James' vein. Van Heerden gave a quick glance to his watch.

Dakota's anger flared, and he started to rush into the room before he caught himself. He checked the time. Only a few more minutes to wait, and the three hours will be up... the incendiaries would —

The sound of shouting filled the night air. "OHEŇ! FEUER! FIRE!"

Van Heerden and the guard dashed out of the room towards the commotion. Dakota couldn't help but smile as he looked to his left, where the flames from the burning outbuilding flickered through the trees.

Dakota surged from the bushes, muscles uncoiling like a cheetah after prey as he burst through the

French doors. A flicker of movement from James drew Dakota's gaze. There was life in him yet.

He pulled out the dagger, the blade slicing cleanly through the binds. As James crumpled, Dakota caught him, grounding his friend's weight against his own sturdy frame. James stirred, a slow return to the waking world marked by a deep inhale and a grimace of pain. He looked at Dakota for a second, confused, as if he didn't know who he was. Then he gave a nod of recognition.

"Let's get out of here," Dakota said. "The raft is on the beach. Now."

James shook his head, a stubborn set to his jaw as he pushed away and stood by himself, having some difficulty keeping his balance. "What time is it?"

Dakota checked his watch. "11:25. Why?"

"We may have time… to stop him." James gasped, brushed past Dakota, and staggered toward the library. He leaned on the doorframe for support. Dakota quickly came behind him to help him stay on his feet.

"What are you talking about?" Dakota asked.

"The broadcast — he's going to do one at midnight. Tonight he's going to initiate the Golden Blight operation. It's our only shot to end it cold," James said. "We have to take it."

James fought off a wave of nausea. Taking a deep breath, he summoned all his strength and pushed off the doorframe. The Golden Blight had to end... tonight. Now.

He entered the office with an unsteady gait and made his way to the shortwave radio. Slumping into the chair in front of it, his fingers traced the list of words on a small piece of paper. It lay next to the pocket watch, its hidden compartment open. Dakota came up next to him. He gripped James' shoulder as though trying to transmit some of his strength.

"Abrogare, morari, ite," James said to himself as he read the slip.

"What are those?" Dakota asked, looking over James's shoulder.

James' voice barely carried above a whisper as he squinted at the writing. "Code words. One for proceed, one to wait, and one to destroy the Golden Blight."

"Which is which?"

"I don't know." James took a deep breath, winced, and closed his eyes.

"Do you recognize what language they are in?"

"Latin."

"Do you speak any Latin?"

"No," James confessed.

Van Heerden burst into the room, his focus solely on the radio until he took a few paces forward and froze in shock. Dakota stood in front of him, eyes blazing with an unbridled fury. Before van Heerden could react, Dakota let out a bestial scream of pure rage and charged towards him. In just two swift steps, he reached van Heerden and viciously latched onto his throat with claw-like fingers.

James strained his eyes, searching for any hint or clue that could help him make sense of the words. His mind was hazy from the effects of the torture battling with the stimulant that had been injected into him.

The sounds of struggle between Dakota and van Heerden behind him only added to his difficulty in focusing. He desperately needed no noise to gather his thoughts and try to remember anything useful.

"Dakota, please! I need quiet!" he barked.

Another punch, the sickening thud of flesh against bone, and then silence. Dakota returned to James's side, breathing heavily.

"Did you..." James' gaze locked onto Dakota's clenched and bruised fists.

"Kill him? No. I almost did, though," Dakota said, his voice hard. "You stopped me."

"Good." James turned back to the list, forcing his mind to focus on the words. He leaned his elbows on the table, running his fingers through his hair. "Abrogare, morari, ite," he said to himself. He shook his head and moaned in defeat. "No, I don't — "

He dropped his right hand. It hit his cross, swinging on the chain around his neck. James automatically grasped it, then... He sat up. A phrase echoed from deep memories, a ghostly chant from his past. "Ite, missa est..."

"What?"

"Ite, missa est... Go, the Mass has ended," James repeated.

"You said you don't speak Latin."

"I don't. But at the orphanage, the Mass was celebrated in Latin." James stopped to take a breath to clear his head. Talking was becoming difficult. "I didn't like not knowing what was being said, so I memorized the Mass in both Latin and English." He gave a weak chuckle. "Smart alack, I guess." He tapped the list. "Ite... go. But that isn't the word I need." He suddenly grabbed the table, steadying himself as the world swayed before his eyes. He groaned.

Dakota put one hand on James' arm. "Come. I need to get you to the medics."

James shook off Dakota's hand. "No! Leave me alone! I will not abandon this! I will figure this out! He will not beat me!" Closing his eyes, he pushed his fists against both sides of his head, as though trying to force the information to emerge.

"Morari... morari..." He sifted through the scattered remnants of text and prayers in his brain. "Animata ecclesia, te invocante moratur... moratur... made to dwell in your presence. Morari... dwell... remain... wait... linger. Not that one either."

He opened his eyes and started at the list. His eyes wouldn't focus completely, but he could barely make out the last word. "Abrogare," he breathed out. "Latin cognate for the English 'abrogate'... nullify... revoke... scrub. Stop. It has to mean stop."

"Are you sure, James?" Dakota gripped his friend's shoulders.

James hesitated. It was time to end the Golden Blight plot once and for all. Or trigger a famine for the West, completely resetting the balance of power in the world. It all depended on if his translation was accurate. After a moment, he reached for the radio dial, his decision made. He managed a grim smile. "I'm going to bet the farm on it."

The distant thump-thump of helicopter blades sliced through the tense silence of the room, quickly followed by the sharp crack of gunfire. James strained against the pain throbbing in his head to focus on the approaching rumble.

"That's the Navy SEALs," Dakota said. "They're coming to lock this place down."

"Time?" James said, his voice barely above a whisper, feeling consciousness slipping like sand through his fingers.

"Five to midnight," Dakota answered after glancing at his watch, then back to James. He squeezed his friend's shoulders tightly. "Hang on, James. Just a little longer."

James nodded, fumbling to switch on the short wave radio set, its dials glowing ominously in the light. Every second, each tick of the clock was a hammer to his skull. He kept pushing back against the haze clouding his mind. He had a mission to finish.

"Tell me when," James' fingers grasped the cold plastic of the transmit switch.

"Midnight. Now!" Dakota's voice cut through the fog in James's mind.

James pressed down on the switch and gathered his strength. "Attention, abrogare. Repeat, abrogare," James said in an authoritative tone, as more gunshots rang out and the chopper came closer. The word transmitted into the ether, a single command that could save or doom them all.

His world narrowed to that moment, the weight of responsibility pressing down until it was all too much. He sat up straight. The room spun sickeningly, like an out-of-control carousel. James hung on for as long as he could, before being thrown off the edge of the world.

Chapter Sixteen

J AMES' EYELIDS FLUTTERED OPEN to a softness that seemed alien after the harsh experiences of... how long ago? He reveled in the comfort of a bed, sinking into the plushness of the linen sheets that felt like a cloud against his skin. Bandages wrapped around his torso, covering the marks of van Heerden's handiwork.

He had no idea how much time had passed. Were he and Dakota successful in stopping van Heerden? Or was he waking to a world of diseased and dying wheat fields?

James couldn't recall ever being in this place before. Sunlight filtered through sheer curtains covering a pair of French doors, casting a warm and inviting glow through the room. Rich oak paneled the walls, giving off a regal and luxurious atmosphere.

The bed was a sumptuous four-poster, fit for royalty. A carved stone mantle stood across from it, projecting a cozy atmosphere. A large and sturdy chest of drawers was against one wall, with a full-length mirror framed in mahogany beside it. Another wall held a slightly open door that revealed a glimpse of the opulent bathroom beyond.

Seated in one of a pair of leather upholstered wing-back chairs flanking the fireplace was a nurse dressed in a crisp white uniform. She was reading a paperback romance novel.

"Uh, hi," James said.

She looked up from her book with a start, her eyes widening in relief. She smiled.

"Oh! You're awake. Good." She checked her watch, picked up a clipboard, and jotted something down. Gathering it up and her novel, she set them on a bedside table. She dialed a few numbers on the bedside phone and spoke in hushed tones. "Mr. Vagus has regained consciousness," she reported.

Before James could ask her any questions, she stepped out of the room. Moments later, Dakota appeared in the doorway and walked to the bed. "Hey, how do you feel?"

"Like I've been run over by a freight train. Several times," James replied, attempting to smile but managing only a grimace. "Groggy."

"You've been under sedation for a few days," Dakota said with a casual shrug. "The doctors decided you needed the rest."

"Van Heerden?" James' voice was urgent now. He struggled to sit upright.

"Smith will fill you in," Dakota said, as he picked up the phone and dialed.

"Okay. Where am I, then?" James asked.

"Smith will tell you that, too," Dakota deflected once more. He spoke into the receiver. "He's awake."

"You're being awfully secretive," James grumbled, crossing his arms across his chest.

"Part of the job description," Dakota said. "Oh, and Aunt Martha gives you her best. How about letting some fresh air into this place?" He walked to the French windows, opened the curtains and doors.

"Wait a minute. Why did the nurse call you first and not Smith?" James challenged.

Dakota took a deep breath of fresh air. "That's better. To answer your question, that favor cost me an expensive, but quite pleasant, dinner."

James gazed at his partner for a moment. "You know, I'm still trying to figure out who the real Dakota is, standing in front of me now. Is he the one who showed such kindness to that bum, or the madman who almost ripped van Heerden apart with his bare hands?"

Dakota faced James, a sly smile on his face. He gave a half-shrug. "Well, we all need a little mystery in our lives. Isn't that right?"

Smith strode into the room, his face glowing with bureaucratic satisfaction. He stood at the foot of James's bed, hands clasped behind his back. "Well, Mr. Vagus. Glad to see you back among us. So you and Mr. Walker turn a simple surveillance assignment into the discovery of a plot set to cripple the food supply of the Western nations," he said without preamble, his voice resonating with authority.

"Sounds like you're fishing for an apology," James shot back.

Smith returned a tight smile. "Hardly. That was an attempt at a compliment. It seems I've been advised to adjust my management style," he said, casting a sidelong glance at Dakota. "But let me tell you the results of your mission. The SEALs secured the island. Van Heerden and Miss Glaum were apprehended and are in federal custody, awaiting trial. Both you and Mr. Walker will undoubtedly be called as witnesses. By the way, Mr. Vagus, I will need you to complete your report of this affair as soon as possible. The prosecutors will require it. I will send up a stenographer."

"Yes, sir," James said.

"Thanks to the efforts of you two — and that recovered book of contacts — a coordinated, international strike force captured all of van Heerden's distributors listed. Their instructions were to hire local personnel to carry out the spreading of the Blight, planned to occur on the twentieth of next month. As a result, Van Heerden's scheme has been demolished, and all vials of the disease have been seized. Oh, Presidential Commendations are in both your files," he added, his tone almost casual, as if such honors were no more extraordinary than a morning cup of coffee. "And word has it other nations intend to express their gratitude. Your actions have spared countless lives."

James and Dakota exchanged grins.

"Also, your exploits have convinced the senators of the intelligence committee who control the purse strings that MIS-X is a viable organization and have fully funded the agency. We are completely operational." Smith beamed.

"I guess we don't have to worry about getting jobs flipping burgers," James said to Dakota with a grin. Dakota returned a thumbs up.

"James also wishes to find out where he is, Mr. Smith," Dakota put in.

"Ah, yes," Smith said, reaching into his side jacket pocket to produce a folded manila envelope. "Your recent charade as a wealthy orphan gave me an idea. MIS-X now owns this sprawling fifty-acre estate along the Upper Hudson River in New York, built in the Gilded Age by a retail tycoon. Ran a chain of five and dime stores.

Now it will be used as our new headquarters and training facility. However, to the outside world, the house and grounds belong to you, a portion of the inheritance from your deceased parents. The story is a detective finally found you after years of searching. Well, that's the thumbnail of the cover. The details are in the envelope. And as is consistent with the modern thought of the younger generation, you have turned your mansion into a commune. Mr. Walker here is your first resident."

"My room is across the hall. I'm supposed to be a potter," Dakota said. "Except every pot I throw turns into an ashtray."

"The cover story will explain the variety of young people arriving and departing," Smith said.

"Although it will irritate the neighbors," James added.

"No doubt," Smith said dryly. "My office will be located elsewhere, and I will pose as the administrator of your trust account." He again glanced between the two teen agents. "I understand that profile has been employed before."

"To great success," Dakota said. James managed not to smile at remembering Dakota's screaming impersonation of Smith over the phone.

James' superior unfolded the manila envelope and handed it to him. "Your role here is crucial, Mr. Vagus.

You must continue to play the part of a rich play-boy. Your new background information is in there. Supporting documentation has already been created and put in place. Memorize every detail of your new identity," he instructed, his tone leaving no room for argument. "Same name. We have created a fictional history that will mesh with your actual one. It's very well done, if I say so myself. It will allow you to tell the sisters at the orphanage about your good fortune. I know they are important to you. So while you recuperate, immerse yourself in the new past we've crafted for you."

"Understood," James replied.

"Again, well done, gentlemen." Smith appeared almost embarrassed at giving two compliments in a such short period. After a curt nod, turned on his heel and exited the room.

Dakota came to attention and saluted the door. "Di... smissed!"

James stared at the envelope he held. "My new iden-tity." He pulled out the contents, sheets of paper, and a few photographs. He glanced at the photos. "They even got pictures of a couple who resemble me. I guess my 'parents'." He slipped the material back into the envelope and took a long look around the bedroom, drinking in the rich details. "My new home." He gave a rueful laugh, then fell silent for a moment. He went on, his voice soft. "I was abandoned on the cold doorstep of the orphanage with nothing but a note pinned to my clothes. It read: 'His name is James.' Those words were the only clue to my identity, but they offered no comfort or explanation. The sisters gave me the last name of Vagus, meaning 'wanderer' in Latin. A fitting one for someone with an unknown past or family, don't you think?"

He paused a second before continuing, his mind searching the vacuum of his past. "I don't know where I was born. I don't know my last name. Parent names: no idea. I don't even know my actual age or birthday. James Vagus' official birth certificate is made up of guesses, estimates, and fabrications." He waved the envelope. "It's as real as what's in here."

Gazing up at the ceiling, he let out a deep sigh. "I waited for years for an adoption to come through," he confessed, his voice filled with longing. "All I ever wanted was someplace to be my home and a family to call my own." His fingers caressed the cross hanging from his neck. "The sisters at the orphanage were wonderful. I love them all, but they're just not the same as a..." The words trailed off. He motioned to the surrounding room. "You know, it's to laugh," he said with no humor. "Now I have a home, but it isn't really mine." He raised the envelope in his hand. "Now I have a family, but it's a phony one."

There was a moment of silence. James became aware that Dakota was gazing at him, as though deciding about something. Dakota walked over to the bed.

"You're wrong on that last point," he said.

James dropped the envelope on the bedspread and looked at Dakota, puzzled.

"Amayeli dayonetli," Dakota held out his hand. "We are brothers."

James smiled and gripped Dakota's hand. "Amayeli dayonetli. We are brothers."